The Science and Technology of Sports

The Science and Technology of FOOTBALL

Melissa Abramovitz

San Diego, CA

© 2020 ReferencePoint Press, Inc.
Printed in the United States

For more information, contact:
ReferencePoint Press, Inc.
PO Box 27779
San Diego, CA 92198
www.ReferencePointPress.com

ALL RIGHTS RESERVED.
No part of this work covered by the copyright hereon may be reproduced or used in any form or by any means—graphic, electronic, or mechanical, including photocopying, recording, taping, web distribution, or information storage retrieval systems—without the written permission of the publisher.

LIBRARY OF CONGRESS CATALOGING-IN-PUBLICATION DATA

Name: Abramovitz, Melissa, 1954– author.
Title: The Science and Technology of Football/by Melissa Abramovitz.
Description: San Diego, CA: ReferencePoint Press, Inc., 2020. | Series: The Science and Technology of Sports | Audience: Grades: 9 to 12. | Includes bibliographical references and index. |
Identifiers: LCCN 2019002666 (print) | LCCN 2019005568 (ebook) | ISBN 9781682826522 (eBook) | ISBN 9781682826515 (hardback)
Subjects: LCSH: Football—Juvenile literature. | Sports sciences—Juvenile literature. | Sports—Technological innovations—Juvenile literature.
Classification: LCC GV950.7 (ebook) | LCC GV950.7 .A28 2020 (print) | DDC 796.332—dc23
LC record available at https://lccn.loc.gov/2019002666

CONTENTS

Introduction   4
Science Affects Everything About Football

Chapter One   8
Physics and Football

Chapter Two   20
Biomechanics and Football

Chapter Three   32
Mind Matters

Chapter Four   44
Science and Football Equipment

Chapter Five   56
Football Injuries

Source Notes   68
For Further Research   72
Index   74
Picture Credits   79
About the Author   80

INTRODUCTION

Science Affects Everything About Football

Most people do not think about science while playing or watching football. But everything about football is about science—lots of science. Areas of science that deal with the shape and structure of the football, the field, the players' minds and bodies, and the weather all influence how the game is played. A few of these scientific disciplines are physics, which describes and explains how physical objects move and interact; kinesiology, the science of movement; biomechanics, a subfield of kinesiology that studies human movement; and psychology, the study of the mind.

A football play called the Mile High Miracle illustrates the interactions between several scientific disciplines. It occurred during a playoff game on January 12, 2013, at the Denver Broncos' Mile High stadium. The Broncos led the Baltimore Ravens 35–28 with forty-one seconds left in the game. Ravens quarterback Joe Flacco launched a 70-yard (64 m) touchdown pass to receiver Jacoby Jones. Elite quarterbacks rarely complete passes that fly more than 50 to 60 yards (45.72 to 54.86 m). But Flacco's height (6 feet 6 inches, or 198 cm), years of fitness and strength training, and thousands of hours of practice made the football zoom over defensive players' heads and land in Jones's hands. Specific skills that worked hand in hand with the laws of phys-

> **physics**
> The science that describes and explains the properties and relationships between physical objects

ics that govern the football's speed, distance, and accuracy included the position of Flacco's feet, his grip on the football's laces, and his ability to quickly calculate how much force and spin he needed to transfer from his muscles to the ball so it would meet Jones's hands at a given moment. As former National Football League (NFL) quarterback Ron Jaworski noted, "That ball dropped out of the sky. And there was only one place the ball could be caught."[1]

The Ravens won the game and went on to defeat the San Francisco 49ers in Super Bowl 47. But the Mile High Miracle was

> **force**
> A source of energy that pushes or pulls something to change its position or motion

Ravens quarterback Joe Flacco throws a 70-yard touchdown pass, dubbed the Mile High Miracle. The distance and accuracy of the pass demonstrate the laws of physics working with Flacco's own physical attributes and skills.

not really a miracle. It resulted from untold hours of coaching, training, and practice that gave the team the tools they needed to translate the sciences of physics, biomechanics, nutrition, and more into a well-played football game.

Math and Football

Many football fans, coaches, and players are not aware that mathematics applies to football. Former San Diego Chargers coach Sid Gillman was one of the first to apply math to team training in the 1960s. Gillman was reportedly frustrated because his players executed plays sloppily no matter how much they practiced. He sent receivers coach Tom Bass to San Diego State College to find out if math professors had any ideas about how to help receivers like Lance Alworth coordinate plays with the quarterbacks.

> **biomechanics**
> The study of how the laws of physics and mechanics affect the ways in which the human body moves

The professors determined that pass patterns could easily be represented by geometry and trigonometry. Specifically, drawing triangles on graph paper provided accurate models of where and how receivers should navigate the field. One side of a triangle represented the receiver's path from the line of scrimmage to a point where he would change direction. The second side represented this new path. It ended at the point where he would catch the football. The third, and longest, side depicted the distance from the quarterback to the appointed catch point. Bass and the professors determined that, ideally, Alworth should complete his run on the first two legs of the triangle at the same time that the quarterback dropped back to pass the football.

The Chargers offense improved dramatically after Bass implemented triangle training. Since then, other coaches have included geometry in football training. In 2013, for example, Dallas Cowboys head coach Jason Garrett started requiring players to understand and use the Pythagorean theorem, which explains the relationship between the sides of a right triangle. Even when players do not consciously use math, experience teaches them that running pass patterns means running triangle shapes.

Science Geeks and Football

In a similar manner, many football players and coaches do not consciously think about the science that underlies the sport, but they still learn to apply the basic principles. They may not know that crouching prevents opponents from imposing a force called torque by lowering an individual's center of mass, but experience teaches them that crouching is the best way to avoid being tackled.

On the other hand, some coaches and players find that learning about and understanding the scientific basis for the sport is beneficial. One such coach was the legendary Vince Lombardi, who coached the two-time Super Bowl–winning Green Bay Packers from 1959 to 1967. Lombardi's experience as a high school science and math teacher before he became a football coach led him to teach his players about the science behind everything they did, and many sports science analysts believe this accounted for much of his success. Indeed, when Lombardi became the Packers' coach in 1959, the team had won only one game that season and was rated the worst in the NFL. Lombardi's ability to teach science and to motivate his team transformed it into one of the most successful teams in NFL history.

CHAPTER ONE

Physics and Football

Physics is the science that describes and explains the qualities, motion, and interactions of physical objects. The motion and interactions of football players with each other, with the football, and with the football field depend on the laws of physics.

Newton's Laws of Motion

The observations and experiments of the British scientist and mathematician Isaac Newton in the mid-1600s to the early 1700s provided the foundation for the fields of modern physics and mechanics. Newton's most famous contributions to science are his three laws of motion, which describe and explain how and why physical objects—such as football players and footballs—move and interact in certain ways. These laws apply to both linear motion, in which an object moves in a straight line, and rotational motion, in which an object spins. Both types of motion play a role in football.

A play that occurred during the first quarter of Super Bowl 53 on February 3, 2019, illustrates how Newton's first law of motion applies to football. It states that an object at rest stays at rest and that an object in motion stays in motion at the same speed and in the same direction unless acted on by an external force. Like all football plays, this one started with the football at rest on the ground. The New England Patriots' center, David Andrews, provided the force that moved the football when he hiked it to quarterback Tom Brady. Brady caught the snap and held the ball in his hands as he prepared to pass it. As he ran around, or scrambled, in the pocket area behind the line of scrimmage while searching for an open receiver, Los Angeles Rams defensive end John Franklin-Myers collided with him and knocked him down. The force Franklin-Myers applied during the collision changed Brady's direction and speed. The force also knocked the football from its resting position in Brady's hands, causing Brady to fumble. As the ball flew out of Brady's hands, the force of gravity interrupted its flight and pulled it toward the ground. After it landed, a force called ground reaction force made it bounce. Andrews then pounced on the ball and provided the force that stopped its bouncing motion.

The forces that influence objects' motion are simply pushes or pulls that can act through direct contact, like a collision, or at a distance, like the force of gravity. Physicists use a measurement called the pound-force, or Newton, to quantify forces. One Newton is the amount of force required to accelerate something with a mass of 35.3 ounces (1 kg) at a rate of 3.28 feet (1 m) per second squared. Acceleration is a measurement of how fast speed changes over time. Mass refers to the number of atoms or the amount of matter something contains. Many people confuse mass with weight, which measures how strongly something is pulled toward the center of the earth by gravity. Things that are more massive typically weigh more than those with less mass, but an object's weight changes when the force of gravity changes. For example, the moon has less gravity than the earth does, so a football player who weighs 250 pounds (113.4 kg) on earth weighs 40 pounds (18.1 kg) on the moon. Mass, on the other hand, stays the same regardless of gravity.

acceleration
A measure of how fast the speed of something is changing

The concepts of potential and kinetic energy are also relevant to Newton's first law. Potential energy is stored energy. When a quarterback lifts a football while preparing to throw it, the work he does by lifting the ball is stored in the ball as potential energy.

Newton's first law of motion is illustrated as quarterback Tom Brady (12) fumbles the football. The force of his collision with the defense changed Brady's direction and speed, while also knocking the football from its resting position.

It can be converted to kinetic energy—the energy of motion—by another force. If the quarterback drops the ball, gravity converts the stored energy to kinetic energy. If the quarterback passes it, force stored in his muscles is transferred to the ball and pushes it forward through the air.

The Law of Inertia

Newton's first law is also called the law of inertia, which is the tendency of an object at rest to remain at rest. The opposite of inertia is momentum, which is the tendency of an object in motion to remain in motion at the same speed in the same direction.

inertia
The resistance of an object to changes in its position or motion

Another Super Bowl 53 play demonstrates that it takes less force to overcome momentum than it does to overcome inertia. Brady directed his first pass at wide receiver Chris Hogan, using force exerted by muscles in his hands, arms, shoulders, torso, legs, and hips to lift the football, pull it back, add spin, and release it. Once the ball was moving and had momentum, all it took for opponent Nickell Robey-Coleman to deflect its path was a tap that sent it away from Hogan and into the hands of Cory Littleton for an interception.

An object's mass also influences inertia and momentum. Thus, more force is needed to start or change the motion of a more massive object than a less massive one. Velocity—the speed and direction of movement—also affects momentum. Newton's second law quantifies this relationship.

Newton's Second Law

Newton's second law states that force equals mass times acceleration. It explains that a force must be applied so an object can accelerate. For example, when a kicker kicks a football, it does not start to accelerate until the kicker's foot provides the force that sends it flying.

A kicker can adjust the amount of force he applies to influence the ball's acceleration. For example, when former collegiate and NFL kicker Alex Henery played for the University of Nebraska, he completed a 57-yard (52.1 m) field goal that set a collegiate record in 2008. Kicking that far required a lot of force, and researchers at the university studied his motion to determine how he did it. Henery loaded potential energy into muscles in his torso, hips, legs, and feet by swinging his kicking leg back and rotating his hip. This caused these muscles to contract, or shorten. When muscles contract, they store potential energy that can be converted to kinetic energy when they lengthen. Henery then ran to the football in its tee on the ground and quickly swung his leg forward. This made the muscles lengthen, and when his foot contacted the ball, it transferred the energy from all those muscles to make the ball sail through the goalposts. Given that the mass of a football is approximately 14.5 ounces (411 g), physicists determined that kicking the field goal required about 137 Newtons of force.

Newton's second law also explains why increased mass helps offensive linemen protect the quarterback during a quarterback sneak. In this play, several large offensive linemen stand side by side to form a wall that prevents defensive players from reaching the quarterback while he sneaks across the goal line for a touchdown. The combined mass of the linemen creates a level of inertia that makes it difficult for opponents, even those

Atlanta Falcons quarterback Matt Ryan carries the football during a play called the quarterback sneak. The combined mass of the offensive linemen who are protecting the quarterback creates a level of inertia that makes it difficult for opponents to break through the line.

who have built up momentum, to move or break through the line. Former NFL quarterback Joey Harrington describes the barrier created by the offensive line as a wave and notes, "You just ride that wave forward."[2]

Newton's Third Law

Newton's third law of motion states that every action has an equal and opposite reaction. For example, when a receiver stands on the field, the amount of force he exerts on the ground equals his weight. This force results from gravity pulling on the person, and as per Newton's third law, the ground exerts an equal force in the opposite direction. This is known as the ground reaction force. When the receiver runs to catch the football, the ground reaction force pushes back on his feet when they touch the ground. Without this push, the receiver could not run because his feet could not overcome the downward force exerted by gravity.

Another instance in which the action-reaction aspect of Newton's third law applies is in collisions between football players. For example, one such collision Green Bay Packers quarterback Aaron Rodgers remembers well occurred in October 2010 during a game against the Washington Redskins. Three defensive tackles collided with and sacked him. The forces each of them exerted on Rodgers were equal to the reactive forces he imposed on each, but since Rodgers was impacted by three separate forces, he took the brunt of the energy involved in the collision.

Even when only two players are involved in a collision, the less massive one is likely to be flattened and/or injured. This fact leads to confusion about Newton's third law. For example, on December 9, 2018, New York Jets defensive linebacker Henry Anderson hit Buffalo Bills kicker Stephen Hauschka, leaving Hauschka with a serious hip injury. Anderson is 6 feet 6 inches (198 cm) tall and weighs 300 pounds (136 kg). Hauschka is 6 feet

4 inches (193 cm) tall and weighs 210 pounds (95.3 kg). Based on Newton's second law, it seems logical that a 300-pound lineman would exert more force than a 210-pound kicker. However, since Newton's third law states that both players experience an equal and opposite force during a collision, many people wonder why this law seems to defy logic.

Physics professor Chad Orzel explains that, in fact, both the second and third laws are valid, and both players experience the same amount of force. It is also true that the less massive player is rattled and injured more often than the more massive one, but not because of the force the player experiences. "What we detect as the sensation of force is actually acceleration, or the change in velocity divided by the duration of the collision,"[3] Orzel writes. In the collision between Hauschka and Anderson, Hauschka experienced approximately 25 percent more acceleration because of his lesser body mass. Thus, his body traveled faster and farther than Anderson's did, and this is why collisions tend to be more traumatic for less massive players.

Conservation of Momentum

Newton's third law also describes and explains the principle of physics known as the law of the conservation of energy. It states that energy cannot be created or destroyed, but it can be transformed into different forms, such as chemical, mechanical, electrical, kinetic, potential, heat, or sound energy. Physicists define energy as the capacity to do work. Work, in turn, is the process of exerting force to change the position or motion of an object.

Football involves many examples of this principle. For instance, the momentum two colliding players bring to a collision is conserved; that is, it stays the same, but its form can change. Indeed, football fans and players are familiar with the partial transformation of momentum to sound energy during collisions. Players' helmets and shoulder pads absorb some of the energy of

Friction: Good, Bad, or Both?

Frictional forces can facilitate or hinder the motion of football players and footballs. Friction occurs because objects like shoes and grass that slide past each other have microscopic ridges and bumps that catch on each other. A type of friction called sliding friction hinders motion, but this is not necessarily a bad thing. Without sufficient friction between players' shoes and the field, players could not run, as evidenced by an icy field reducing friction. The amount of sliding friction increases in objects with more mass and with rough surfaces. A more massive player wearing shoes with cleats, for example, creates more friction than a less massive one with no cleats.

The friction between a layer of liquid, such as ice or water, and another object is called lubricated friction. The lubricating layer reduces the amount of friction, which is good if someone is wearing skis on a snow-packed mountain. In football, however, lubricated friction makes it difficult to run or change direction.

Aerodynamic drag is another type of friction. It occurs when air molecules crash into a flying object like a football, slowing the object's motion. The amount of drag increases as the object's speed and size increase. This is why quarterbacks add spin when they pass a football. Spin keeps the ball moving nose first, and the drag is less than it would be if a wider part of the football led its motion.

motion, and the rest is released in the form of sound waves that are described as snap, crackle, pop, boom, and thud.

Physics, Luck, and the Immaculate Reception

Newton's third law is linked to one of the most famous and hotly debated plays in professional football. Known as the Immaculate Reception, it took place on December 23, 1972, at Three Rivers Stadium in Pittsburgh during a league play-off game between the Oakland Raiders and the Pittsburgh Steelers. With 22 seconds left in the game, Oakland led with a score of 7–6, and Pittsburgh faced a fourth down on its own 40-yard line. After the snap, Raiders defensive players pushed through the Steelers' offensive line and were about to sack Steelers quarterback Terry Bradshaw as he prepared to throw a pass to receiver John Fuqua. Bradshaw launched the football, and a split second before Fuqua caught it, Raiders safety Jack Tatum knocked him down. The ball bounced off Tatum and flew backward toward Steelers fullback Franco Harris, who caught it right before it hit the ground. Harris outmaneuvered Raiders who moved to tackle him and made a touchdown, winning the game.

Observers argued about whether the touchdown was legitimate, with some claiming the ball touched Fuqua rather than Tatum. Had it hit Fuqua before Harris caught it, it would have been an incomplete pass according to NFL rules. The issue was widely debated, and film of the game is unfocused, so no one could determine what actually happened—until physics professor John Fetkovich analyzed the game film and concluded that Newton's third law proved the ball had indeed struck Tatum. Fetkovich explained that the film was clear enough to see the numbers on the players' uniforms and the direction the ball flew after it bounced off Tatum's shoulder. He noted that the ball's path when it flew backward resulted from the conservation of Tatum's momentum that was transferred to the ball. Had the ball hit Fuqua, who was running across the field, it would have rebounded in a direction opposite to that of Fuqua's momentum.

A Steelers fan named Michael Ord first used the name Immaculate Reception when he was out celebrating the Steelers win after the game. The phrase is a pun that refers to the Catholic dogma of the Immaculate Conception. However, Raiders players, coaches, and fans who disagreed with the referees' decision still call the play the Immaculate Deception.

Other Physics Concepts

Other concepts of physics that are important in football are center of mass—also called center of gravity—torque, and power. Center of mass is the place on an object at which its mass is concen-

Running back Darren Sproles (43) outmaneuvers the defense. His smaller stature and lower center of gravity make him much quicker than larger opponents and harder to tackle.

trated and at which the force of gravity acts the most. Torque is a force that makes an object spin, and power is the rate at which energy is expended.

NFL running back Darren Sproles's performance depends on these three concepts. Sproles's center of mass is lower than that of most professional football players because he is 5 feet 6 inches (168 cm) tall and weighs 190 pounds (86.2 kg). The center of mass on a human is below the rib cage, near the navel. Smaller people naturally have a lower center of gravity, and this gives players like Sproles built-in stability that enhances the ability to quickly run, change direction, and maneuver around

How Would Football Change If We Changed the Laws of Physics?

We cannot change the laws of physics. But physics professor Chad Orzel wrote a fun article about what might happen in football if we could.

Making Earth's gravity as weak as that on Mars would pull objects toward Earth's center with an acceleration of 12.2 feet (3.7 m) per second squared instead of 32.2 feet (9.8 m) per second squared. "With weaker gravity, a quarterback could fling the ball farther down the field, and a receiver could leap higher in search of a catch," Orzel wrote. Less gravity would also reduce the force and friction from players' feet pressing against the ground, making them hop instead of run.

Orzel says reducing the speed of light from 983,571,056 feet (299,792,458 m) per second to 49.2 feet (15 m) per second would produce "utter chaos" because of Einstein's principle of special relativity. It states that since light travels at a constant speed for everyone, perceptions of time and size vary depending on individuals' positions and speed of motion.

Chaos from special relativity might look like this: A quarterback scrambling in the pocket hurries to pass the football because he believes only five seconds remain in the game. He aims at a receiver who appears to be 10 yards (9.1 m) away in the end zone. At the same time, the receiver sprints downfield to cover the 35 yards (32 m) between himself and the end zone before the clock runs out in twenty-six seconds.

Chad Orzel, "Football Physics: How Would Changing the Laws of Physics Change Football?," *Forbes*, November 22, 2015. www.forbes.com.

opponents. Coupled with power gained through fitness training and conditioning, Sproles is known for being fast and elusive on the field. Sportswriter Chris B. Brown calls him a "runner/receiver/kick returner/human Molotov cocktail."[4]

When an opponent catches Sproles, his low center of gravity makes it difficult to tackle him. Coaches teach football players to tackle opponents by applying torque to areas on the opponent's lower body, such as the legs, that are farthest from the center of mass. The farther from the center of gravity torque is exerted, the less force is needed to rotate and topple the object. Coaches teach larger players to lower their center of mass by crouching low and firmly planting their feet to become as tackle resistant as possible.

Training to consistently lower one's center of mass is just one way in which football players learn to use principles of physics to their advantage. Although it is difficult to predict some aspects of the game, such as what an opposing team's next play will be, one thing players can rely on is that everything either team does will be governed by these principles.

CHAPTER TWO

Biomechanics and Football

Biomechanics experts study how principles of physics and mechanical engineering apply to human movement. These principles govern everything football players do, just like they describe and explain the motion of objects. Analyzing how muscles, bones, and other body parts work together to allow a kicker to launch a field goal or a running back to outmaneuver a lineman can help coaches develop effective training programs, and biomechanical analyses can even demonstrate why spectators are incorrect when they assume it is easy to throw a gracefully arcing pass that falls right into a receiver's hands. Indeed, an analysis of former NFL quarterback Jimmy Clausen's passes shows why physicist and former football coach Larry McDaniel calls passing "the toughest motor skill to learn"[5] in any sport.

Mastering the complex chain of motions that constitutes a football pass takes years of practice because perfect timing, technique, and body alignment are critical. Clausen perfected his passes by practicing every element in slow motion when he was a high school quarterback in Westlake Village, California, a collegiate standout at Notre Dame University, and in the NFL from 2010 to 2015.

After taking the snap, Clausen firmly plants his back foot to serve as an anchor. He then takes his left hand off the football as the fingers on his right hand gently grip the ball across its laces. He tucks his left elbow against his rib cage while cocking his right arm back and above his right ear. Keeping his right elbow above his shoulder at a 90-degree angle as his arm swings forward to launch the ball, he rotates his shoulder and hips as his pinky finger leaves the ball first, followed by his ring, middle, and index fingers. As his index finger leaves the ball, he snaps his wrist. This leaves his palm facing outward in what kinesiologists call a supination of the hand. In the final motion, Clausen's right arm straightens across his body with the thumb pointing downward.

The Musculoskeletal System

Every bodily system contributes to performing skills like passing, but the musculoskeletal and cardiovascular systems play the most significant roles. The musculoskeletal system consists of bones, muscles, and the muscles' connections to the nervous system.

Skeletal muscles are made of bundles of two main types of muscle cells: slow-twitch (ST) and fast-twitch (FT) fibers. These cells, which are collectively called myocytes, in turn contain strands called myofibrils that can stretch and contract. When bundles of myocytes contract or stretch, this activates entire muscles, which pull on ligaments and tendons to move bones in ways that allow people to move around and perform other actions. Ligaments are cartilage structures that attach bones to each other, and tendons are similar structures that attach muscles to bones. Muscles become active in response to biochemical and electrical instructions from nerve cells, or neurons, in the brain and spinal cord. The sequence of events that follows a quarterback's desire to throw a football illustrates how this happens. First, neurons in the quarterback's brain signal his intention to motor neurons in the spinal cord that regulate the biceps, brachialis, and brachioradialis muscles in his throwing arm. These muscles respond by pulling on tendons and ligaments

myocytes
Muscle fiber cells

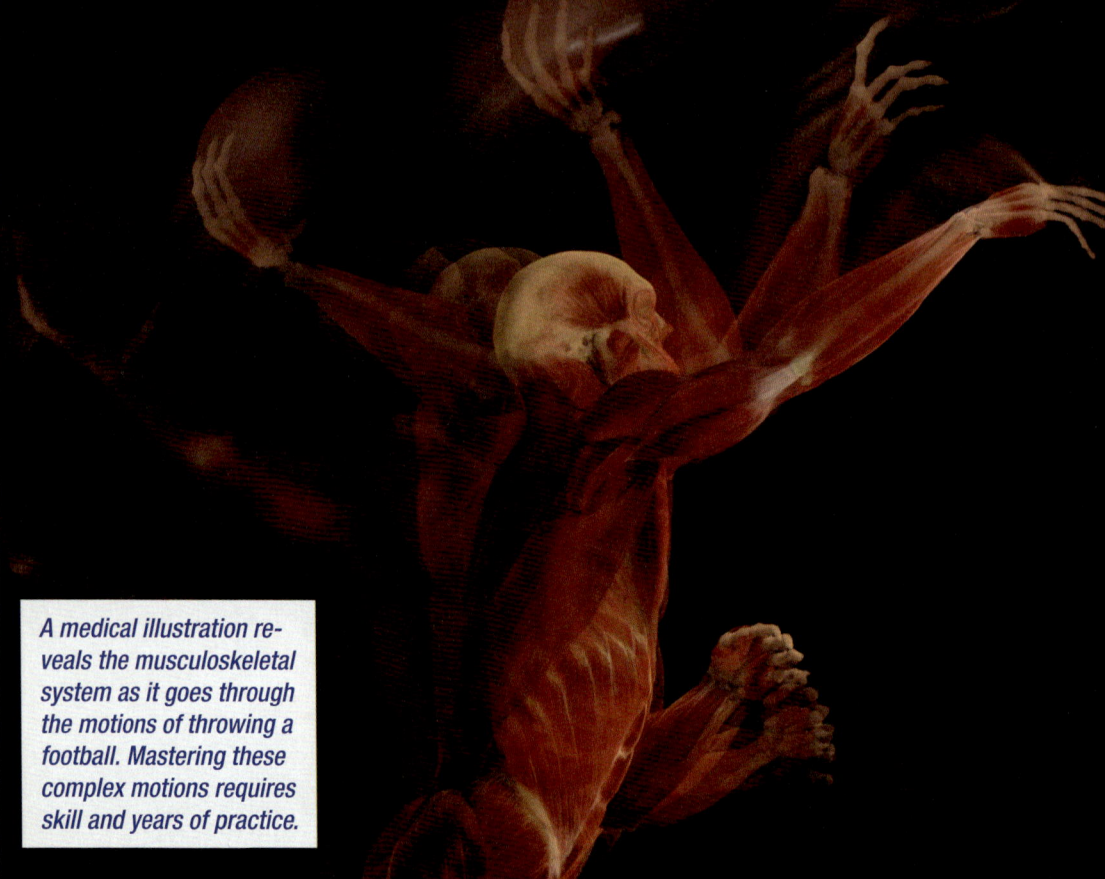

A medical illustration reveals the musculoskeletal system as it goes through the motions of throwing a football. Mastering these complex motions requires skill and years of practice.

connected to the humerus, radius, and ulna bones. This causes the elbow joint to bend. When the quarterback wants to release the football, motor neurons that control the triceps muscle signal it to straighten the elbow joint. Of course, the action is more complicated than this because muscles throughout the quarterback's body, in addition to those in his arm, participate.

Energy and Muscle

The neuron-muscle activation system would not work without the energy that the muscles use to generate the forces they need to move. Muscles obtain this energy by converting chemical energy to mechanical energy aerobically, meaning with oxygen, or anaerobically, meaning without oxygen. Different types and durations of activities rely on muscle cells using different processes to produce the fuel they convert to energy. This fuel is called adenosine triphosphate (ATP).

> **adenosine triphosphate (ATP)**
> The fuel that powers muscles

Muscle cells produce enough energy to last for approximately ten seconds by converting a chemical called phosphocreatine into ATP. Phosphocreatine comes from food and is stored in muscle cells. When muscles need additional energy, FT fibers use the process of glycolysis to make ATP from glucose, or sugar. Glycolysis provides enough energy to last about two minutes, which is why FT fibers are ideally suited for generating short bursts of energy. When more energy is needed, ST fibers take oxygen from the blood and convert it to ATP by burning fat and glucose that are stored in muscle cells. This aerobic process provides energy for long-term activities like distance running.

After muscle cells produce ATP, they convert the resulting potential energy into the kinetic energy needed for their activities, based on instructions from motor neurons. The amount and intensity of the neural signals influence the force they exert. For example, if a motor neuron fires once, the associated muscle fibers twitch. If it fires repeatedly, this activates more FT muscle fibers. FT fibers produce more force than ST fibers because FT fibers contain more ATPase, which is an enzyme that breaks down ATP. The more ATP that is broken down, the more kinetic energy the muscle has.

Most plays in football last less than a minute, so football players focus on training that enhances activation of FT fibers. NFL running back Adrian Peterson, for example, promotes efficient FT fiber activation by doing 50, 75, and 100-yard (45.7, 68.6, and 91.4 m) sprints with and without resistance. The resistance comes from dragging a weighted sled—a cart that can be loaded with weights. This type of exercise translates to the ability to engage in explosive, powerful moves in football games.

The Cardiovascular System

The cardiovascular system, which consists of the heart, lungs, and blood vessels, also adapts to regular workouts by becoming more efficient. One cardiovascular function is taking in oxygen through the nose and mouth and sending it to the lungs, where millions of tiny sacs called alveoli transfer it to the bloodstream. The heart and blood vessels send this oxygenated blood to cells and tissues throughout the body. After cells use oxygen, blood vessels carry carbon dioxide, the waste gas that remains, to the lungs, which exhale it through the nose and mouth.

The cardiovascular system adapts to regular exercise by more efficiently pumping blood to muscles and increasing the lungs' ability to extract oxygen from air that is breathed in. These adaptations are especially useful for endurance activities, such as running 90 yards (82.3 m) for a touchdown, but also benefit athletes who need energy for multiple short-term explosive moves. For example, NFL linemen, which include offensive and defensive safeties, tackles, and blockers, participate in an average of sixty-five plays per game. Although most plays last less than a minute, each involves tremendous exertions of force and power that make endurance necessary. In fact, when 49ers general manager Trent Baalke first saw defensive lineman DeForest Buckner play for the University of Oregon, Baalke was most impressed by Buckner's stamina, especially after learning that Buckner played during 951 snaps in the 2015 season. This played a role in the 49ers decision to draft Buckner in 2016.

calories
The energy provided by food; stored in the human body as chemical potential energy

Diet and Athletes

Muscles and other body parts depend on an athlete's diet to furnish the nutrients they need to produce energy and enhance fitness and football skills. The cascade of energy transformation begins with the body transforming food energy into chemical potential energy and storing it in body cells. Calories measure food energy and are

Rocky Mountain High

The mile-high (1.6 km) football stadium in Denver, Colorado, illustrates how the number of air molecules, or air density, affects players' ability to function. As elevation increases, air density decreases. This means the air gets thinner. Thinner air has fewer oxygen molecules, and people's lungs therefore take in and distribute less oxygen to body cells. People who are not used to higher elevations therefore experience breathing difficulties and fatigue. "You feel yourself gasping," explains Patriots linebacker Tedy Bruschi. Physicists calculated that air contains about 700 billion trillion molecules per cubic foot at sea level. The density in Denver is about 20 percent lower than this number.

It takes humans about eighteen days to adjust to higher elevations. Those who regularly live and work at high altitudes, such as Denver Broncos football players, breathe fine because their bodies adjust by producing more red blood cells, which carry oxygen to body cells. This gives the Broncos an advantage over visiting teams. As former Broncos coach John Fox put it, living and training in Denver gives the team "probably the best home-field advantage in the NFL."

Indeed, the Broncos have won more home games than any other NFL team, which is why many NFL players dread playing in Denver. Patriots quarterback Tom Brady is especially wary of visiting Denver because his team has lost seven games and won only two against the home-field Broncos. This led journalists to call the Broncos stadium Brady's "personal House of Horrors."

Quoted in Brandon Hall, "Denver's Edge: How Altitude Provides Their Teams with the Greatest Home-Field Advantage in Sports," Stack, December 8, 2017. www.stack.com.

---

defined as the amount of heat needed to raise the temperature of 1 gram (1/3 oz) of water 1 degree Celsius (2 degrees F). Muscle cells convert stored calories and nutrients to ATP and transform ATP into kinetic energy. According to sports nutritionists, a 300-pound (136 kg) lineman can use as many as 2,000 calories during a football game. Many adults consume less than this number of calories each day. However, large elite football players may consume 9,000 to 10,000 calories per day without gaining weight because they expend so many calories in practices and games.

Besides supplying football players with sufficient calories, nutritionists and team trainers make sure they consume adequate amounts of protein, found in meats, dairy products, and nuts; carbohydrates, found in bread, pasta, rice, fruits, and vegetables; and fats, found in most protein foods and oils, to repair damaged tissue, maintain muscle energy stores, and keep body organs functioning optimally. In one interview, offensive linemen on the Northwestern University football team noted that their trainers and nutritionists require them to consume at least 80 percent of their calories in the form of healthy foods.

Training and Conditioning

The nutrients and calories football players ingest allow them to engage in the training and conditioning programs and skills-training drills that prepare them for their roles on a team. Programs that emphasize training for specific qualities such as strength and speed, as well as overall fitness and stamina, produce the best results. Indeed, studies by football analyst Josh Hermsmeyer and other researchers indicate that teams and/or individuals whose training skimps on overall fitness and stamina have difficulties performing consistently in a game that routinely lasts three or more hours. These studies also show that in general, NFL players run more slowly and otherwise perform less optimally during the fourth quarter than they do earlier in the game.

This is why strength and conditioning coaches who emphasize overall fitness tend to produce winning teams. One example is the New England Patriots, whose coaches demand that players run up hills after they are exhausted from practicing for hours at training camp. The players state that they hate those hills; receiver Danny Amendola called one of them "a beast, for sure," and others talk about "those [bleeping] hills."[6] But the players admit that they like the results. When other teams are fatigued and getting sloppy during the fourth quarter, the Patriots regularly make remarkable comebacks to win games in which they trailed

Collegiate football players stretch and warm up before playing. Strength-training and conditioning coaches emphasize overall fitness, which has been proven to improve players' stamina and performance.

an opponent by as many as 20 points. According to sportswriter Kevin Clark, "New England's ability to come back from impossible odds is directly tied to [the running.]"[7]

Training for Strength and More

Besides building good endurance, football training and conditioning programs include exercises that build other important qualities. One such quality is strength, which is defined as the maximum force an athlete can exert against resistance, such as barbells and weights. A muscle's size influences the amount of force it can produce; biomechanics experts find that muscles can exert approximately 63 Newtons of force per square millimeter of muscle area.

One way to strengthen muscles is by enlarging them. This is often done by lifting increasingly heavy weights. This leads to

27

Explosive Power

One NFL player who works tirelessly to achieve the power, agility, and quickness that underlie his football skills is defensive end J.J. Watt. At 6 feet 5 inches (195.6 cm) tall, Watt is known for exploding off the line of scrimmage and sacking quarterbacks, among other talents. In 2015, when Watt was honored as the first NFL player to achieve twenty or more quarterback sacks in one season, sportswriter Brandon Hall noted that "Watt's unique blend of power, agility, and explosiveness is once again terrorizing NFL offenses," and added that Watt is often described as "an avalanche inside a tornado."

Another of Watt's nicknames, J.J. Swat, derives from his ability to bat down or intercept passes before they reach the intended receiver. This ability depends on having quick hands, which he says he developed playing hockey during his youth. These days, he enhances his quickness by standing in front of a football-throwing machine that spits out footballs traveling approximately 40 miles (64.4 km) per hour and grabbing the footballs with one hand as they whiz past him. He builds quickness and agility in his feet and legs by doing shuffle drills, which involve moving quickly from side to side while frequently changing direction. Plyometrics such as long jumps and box jumps—jumping onto a box after squatting—help him enhance his power.

Jeff Beckham, "Science Turns the NFL's J.J. Watt into a Tower of Power," *Wired*, October 7, 2015. www.wired.com.

Brandon Hall, "Football Film Room: Breaking Down a J.J. Watt Sack," Stack, November 27, 2015. www.stack.com.

---

tiny tears in muscle fibers, and the damage causes the body to release chemicals called growth factors. Growth factors cause satellite cells outside muscle fibers to reproduce and fuse with existing muscle fibers, which results in increased muscle size. However, enlarging muscles too much can backfire because overly large muscles interfere with other important qualities like quickness, power, flexibility, and agility.

Quickness is the ability to react fast to a stimulus, such as the sight of a defensive tackle about to throw a player to the ground, so as to immediately perform an action like changing speed or direction. Closely related to quickness is agility, which is the ability to quickly change speed and/or direction while keeping the body stable and balanced. Agility largely depends on having a strong core, the muscles in the abdomen that influence posture and balance, and flexibility is the ability to stretch the muscles without pain.

Lineman Training

Power, quickness, agility, flexibility, and balance are important for all football players, but many people who believe linemen are simply big, strong brick walls are surprised to learn that elite linemen excel in all these qualities. Los Angeles Rams defensive lineman Aaron Donald, who is 6 feet 1 inch (185.4 cm) and weighs 280 pounds (127 kg), excels even more than most.

Donald is known for using these attributes to disrupt opponents' passing, running, and kicking plays, and words like *dreaded* and *nightmare* are often used to describe him. Sportswriter Mark Bullock of the *Washington Post*, for example, called him "a nightmare for offensive coordinators to game-plan against in all facets of the game. He is someone they have to be able to identify and base their plans around each and every play."[8]

Assigning multiple players to block and/or run Donald out of bounds usually fails to stop him. For example, in a game against the Minnesota Vikings in October 2018, Donald broke away from guard Tom Compton, then pushed aside center Pat Elflein and sacked quarterback Kirk Cousins for a 10-yard (9.1 m) loss. In another play, he again sacked Cousins after maneuvering around the guard, tackle, and center who were assigned to block him.

One aspect of training for the type of power and maneuverability that Donald possesses involves performing traditional strength-training exercises quickly. Craig Fitzgerald, the head strength coach for the Houston Texans, incorporates this type

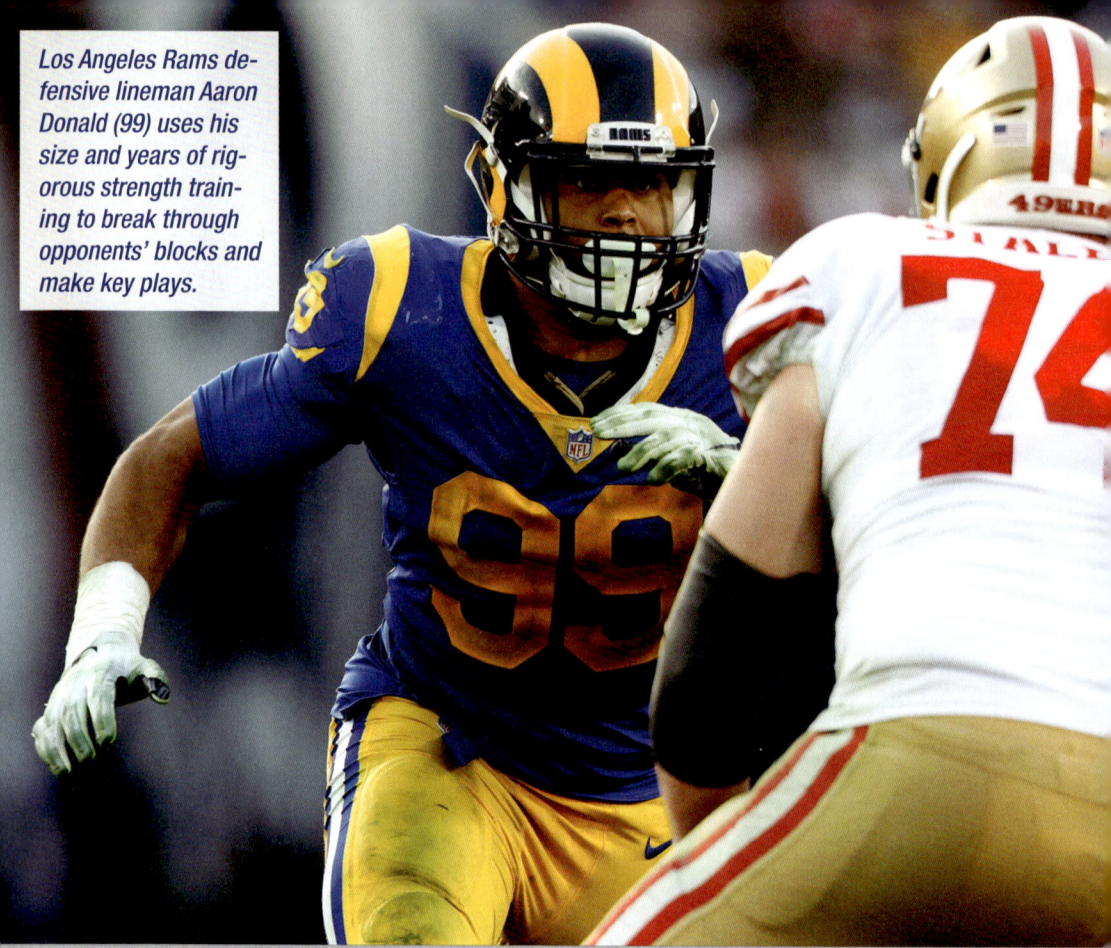

Los Angeles Rams defensive lineman Aaron Donald (99) uses his size and years of rigorous strength training to break through opponents' blocks and make key plays.

of exercise into his conditioning program for linemen. "Make the weights rattle on squats," he tells his players. "If you're not moving the weights fast, it's not going to transfer to the field. It doesn't matter how much weight you can squat slowly, it matters how much weight you can move fast."[9] Linemen also enhance their skills by pushing and pulling exercise sleds loaded with weights.

Skills Training

Another part of training for a specific position entails skills drills. For instance, quarterbacks practice various aspects of passing, scrambling, and running again and again until these skills become second nature. If a quarterback needs work on a specific skill like coordinating his footwork and arm motions, trainers and coaches help the player break these motions down so he can practice each individually before combining them.

Quarterback Joe Flacco combines skills drills with conditioning exercises that help him perform these skills. For example, he does neck flexing exercises, barbell shrugs, hand and finger exercises, and overhead presses with weights to improve his grip on the football and increase the power of his throwing arm. He also incorporates advice from his coaches and trainers into his skills training. After quarterbacks coach Jim Caldwell noticed that Flacco could add force to his passes by bending his knees more, he taught Flacco how to store additional energy in his knees and transfer it to the football when he released it.

Even though the cells, muscles, and other human body parts are more complex than the nonliving elements of the sport, the same principles of physics apply to both. However, unlike inanimate objects, football players can optimize the biomechanics of their movements through practice, conditioning, and training.

CHAPTER THREE

Mind Matters

Mental qualities such as motivation, dedication, concentration, and self-confidence are as important, if not more so, than physical qualities like strength and speed in creating outstanding players and teams that consistently excel. Indeed, when asked why Patriots quarterback Tom Brady was selected by his peers as one of the best NFL players every year between 2011 and 2018, most of his teammates and opponents alike said that Brady's mental strength led them to vote for him. "He stays calm and he just does his job,"[10] stated Raiders quarterback Derek Carr.

Players themselves are responsible for developing positive mental qualities, but those around them also have a huge effect on this process. Some athletes consult sports psychologists to help them maximize their drive and competitive edge. Others benefit from teammates, coaches, and trainers who exert positive influences. Many coaches, in fact, consider their primary responsibility to be nurturing players' mental strength so they are motivated to work hard to become better athletes than they thought they could ever be.

Motivation Magic

Chris Carlisle is a strength and conditioning coach widely known for motivating and inspiring his players through his passion for helping them be their best. "Every day I get to make players better. I've been involved in coaching for 31 years, and I think of myself as a service to our players, helping them accomplish their dreams,"[11] Carlisle stated in a 2015 interview with newspaper reporters in his hometown of Mason City, Iowa. He is also known for inspiring players with his courage and commitment. In 2001, when he coached at the University of Southern California, he was fighting a cancer called Hodgkin's lymphoma. He did not tell his team, except for head coach Pete Carroll, about his illness until after his doctors told him he was in remission. He was nominated for numerous courage awards as a result, and his players often commented about his lasting effects on their character and motivation to always put forth maximum effort.

Like Carlisle, many coaches and trainers teach positive mental skills by setting good examples. Collegiate football coach Keith Grabowski states that one way to set a good example that builds a team's motivation and confidence is to make pregame talks positive. Mentioning anything negative, including referring to a past loss or to any type of revenge, he states, sets a poor example and is liable to shatter rather than build team loyalty.

The late Packers coach Vince Lombardi is often referred to as the strongest motivator in football history, and a famous championship game called the Ice Bowl illustrates the power of his attitude and influence. The game between the Packers and Cowboys occurred on December 31, 1967, when the temperature in Green Bay, Wisconsin, was -15°F (-26°C). The icy field and the effects of the cold, such as frostbite, made moving around difficult, and most people thought the young, talented Cowboys would win against the still competitive but aging Packers. As Cowboys defensive end George Andrie later stated, "We knew we were better than they were."[12]

Against these odds, Lombardi's lessons in motivation and hard work helped the Packers rise above the difficult conditions. With four minutes left in the game, the Cowboys led 17–14, and the Packers had the ball. Quarterback Bart Starr calmly led the team to the Cowboys' 3-yard line and scored using a quarterback sneak. The Packers' public relations director, Chuck Lane, states that the entire team viewed this win as a tribute to Lombardi. It was, Lane says, "the essence of Lombardi. . . . He willed victory with his strength of character and all he stood for—precision, hard work, the simplification of roles."[13]

Dedication, Confidence, and Focus

Closely related to motivation are the dedication, confidence, and focus that help individuals and teams shine in a competitive game in which everyone at the collegiate and professional levels is an outstanding athlete. There are many examples of players with run-of-the-mill physical talent who become superstars due to these attributes. One such player is quarterback Peyton Manning. Football coach Travis Brody describes Manning as "not a great athlete, lacks any kind of real speed, has below average arm strength for an NFL quarterback and is not particularly accurate compared to guys like Tom Brady, Drew Brees, or Aaron Rodgers." But Brody says that Manning became a first-rate quarterback because he studied film for hours and otherwise

Peyton Manning (center) calls a play in a huddle. Manning's work ethic and his dedication, confidence, and focus helped him become one of the NFL's top quarterbacks.

prepared for games in ways that made him "mentally superior to almost anyone on the field."[14]

Psychologists note that the ability to focus on the task at hand is among the most important determinants of success. It is so important that football players often try to distract or intimidate opponents to disrupt their ability to concentrate. This is known as mental warfare. Some football players are in fact known for unceasingly tormenting opponents with trash talk or other methods of distraction. Athletes who learn to ignore or otherwise remove themselves mentally from this type of mental warfare find that this gives them a huge competitive edge.

However, many players say it is difficult to ignore mental warfare and/or intimidation. Former Packers quarterback Brett Favre often spoke about how Tampa Bay Buccaneers defensive tackle Warren Sapp, who Favre called "the king of trash talk,"[15] taunted opponents before, during, and after plays. Sapp himself explained that he aimed to distract opponents so they performed badly and became angry enough to pick fights. "That was my domain. I had a masters degree and two doctorates in this,"[16] Sapp says jokingly.

Another renowned trash talker, the Raiders' Lester Hayes, thoroughly researched opponents when choosing his targets. He then frightened these targets by threatening to harm their wives and children. He also punched opponents in the neck or other body parts to really scare them, even though this is against the rules. The Raiders' well-known obsession with winning made him and his teammates willing to do anything necessary to gain a competitive edge.

A more civilized type of mental warfare involves faking out an opponent. This is a good way to disrupt the opposing team's concentration by introducing an unexpected twist. There have been many well-known fake outs in football. One that Michigan State University (MSU) coach Mark Dantonio dubbed Little Giants occurred on September 18, 2010, when the MSU Spartans were trailing the Notre Dame Fighting Irish by three points and had a fourth-down situation on the Irish 29-yard line during overtime. Everyone expected MSU kicker Dan Conroy to attempt a 46-yard field goal to tie up the score. But Dantonio called for the Little Giants fake out the team had practiced. Punter Aaron Bates, who was the ball holder for Conroy, took the snap. Conroy got out of the way, and tight end Charlie Gantt sprinted downfield. Bates stepped to his right and launched a 29-yard spot-on pass that Gantt caught and ran in for a touchdown, with no defensive players anywhere nearby. A Bleacher Report article predicted that "Little Giants will be talked about for generations; a fearless call when things mattered most."[17] Indeed, it is among the most acclaimed instances of beautifully played deception in college football history.

Motor Learning

Motor learning is another mental process that is important for sports performance. It helps athletes transform consciously executed skills into reflexes, or motor learning programs, that occur automatically, without the need to consciously think about each step. Motor learning develops from external feedback from coaches and trainers and internal feedback that muscles and other body parts send to the brain when a skill is practiced.

One important aspect of motor learning is that it contributes to fast reaction times. A reaction time is the length of time it takes an individual to respond to a stimulus. Quick reaction times are critical for football players, and reducing players' reaction times can mean the difference between winning or losing a game. Athletes used to reduce their reaction times by simply practicing skills, but virtual reality (VR) technologies are now being used with old-fashioned practice to hasten the positive effects. In 2016 the Clemson University football team began using a VR program that immerses users in

> **motor learning**
> Training the brain to automatically execute the motions that make up complex motor skills

Football Players Can Feel Afraid and Alone

The importance of mental and emotional health to playing competitive football and the prevalence of depression and other mood disorders in football players is reflected in the Carolina Panthers' management decision to hire a full-time psychotherapist, Tish Guerin, in 2018. The Panthers were the first professional football team to do so. Previously, Panthers employees could consult a mental health doctor when needed, but no such professional was on the organization's staff.

Many coaches and players have applauded this change as a step forward in acknowledging the importance of mental health and in diminishing the stigma of asking for help. Many people, particularly men who view themselves as tough guys, are especially unlikely to seek help for mental and emotional problems. But Guerin's presence, along with increased public education about mental health, is changing the Panthers' attitudes.

Steve Smith, a top Panthers receiver from 2001 to 2013, was one of the few players to seek mental health help before the team hired Guerin. However, he did not speak publicly about his struggles with depression until 2018, when he admitted that he felt "trapped, inferior, and alone" during his football career. He stated that Guerin's presence helped him come forward because it proved that talking about emotional challenges is no longer viewed as shameful or weak.

Quoted in David Newton, "Panthers' Hiring of a Mental Health Clinician Is a 'Game Changer,'" ESPN, November 7, 2018. www.espn.com.

game situations taken from real-life films and allows them to practice relevant moves over and over. That year, quarterback Deshaun Watson led the team to its first National Collegiate Athletic Association championship since 1981. While preparing for the championship game against the University of Alabama, Watson focused on immersing himself in hundreds of VR scenarios that helped him quickly identify and respond to blitzes—plays in which more than four defensive players rush the quarterback—because Alabama is known for blitzing. Watson notes that this taught him "to react without thinking"[18] during the game, which led him to complete six out of seven passes during the fourth quarter. Two of those passes led to touchdowns.

Unlearning Motor Learning

Along with the benefits of motor learning comes the challenging characteristic that once a motor learning program is in place, it is very difficult to unlearn or reverse it. Thus, if an athlete learns to perform a skill incorrectly, it is more difficult for him or her to unlearn and replace it than it would be to learn a new skill. Quarterback Aaron Rodgers is familiar with this difficulty because coaches during his high school and college football years taught him to hold the football incorrectly. He held it too high up, at ear height, and too far behind him, giving him an awkward backward lean. This caused him to jerk his arm awkwardly and to release the ball inconsistently. When he was drafted into the NFL in 2005, he had to learn the correct biomechanics. This took countless hours of focused effort and practice but resulted in a smoother arm motion that greatly enhanced the accuracy of his passes.

Neuroscientists at the University of California, Santa Barbara, and the Michigan Institute of Technology discovered that the neurological basis for this difficulty is that neurons called tonically active neurons (TANs) in the brain's striatum create very durable memories that are resistant to being erased. The researchers call the striatum the part of the brain "where skills and habits meet"[19] and note that one method of getting TANs to remove the biochemical locks they place on these memories is to begin relearning a particular behavior in a different environment than the one in which the behavior was originally learned.

resilience
The ability to overcome setbacks

Resilience

The mental quality of resilience also facilitates skill learning and relearning, and in addition it heavily influences athletes' self-confidence, motivation, and overall performance. Another term for *resilience* is *mental toughness*. Resilient people bounce back from mistakes or disappointments and use these events as learning experiences. Sports psychologist Mike Edger writes that athletes who continue to focus on mistakes often see their performance decline because someone who is focused on the past is not focused on the present. "A resilient athlete is one who is able to overcome setbacks, remain confident, and focus on the present,"[20] states Edger.

Baltimore Ravens placekicker Justin Tucker is an example of a resilient player. In 2018 Tucker was named the most accurate kicker in NFL history. He had never missed a post-touchdown extra point conversion until October 21, 2018, with twenty-four seconds left in a game against the New Orleans Saints, who won the game.

The miss was not Tucker's fault. He had launched the kick as he always did, but just before it sailed through the goalposts, a

Baltimore Ravens placekicker Justin Tucker kicks a field goal. Tucker's resilience, motivation, and fine-tuned skills helped him earn the title of the most accurate kicker in NFL history.

powerful gust of wind sent it in another direction. Indeed, a newspaper article about the game stated that "the wind was treacherous."[21] But Tucker still felt that he had let down his team.

His resilience and dedication to football, coupled with emotional support from his teammates and coaches, helped him quickly put the incident behind him. After the game, he told reporters he would "let this hurt for another couple of hours . . . [but

The Hail Mary Pass and Motor Learning Programs

Many times, players who have reached the point of not having to consciously think about the steps involved in executing certain skills are not aware of just how thoroughly their brain-to-body control system is programmed to automatically do the right thing. The Hail Mary pass, which is deeply entrenched in football folklore, is a type of play that illustrates how powerful these subconscious motor skills programs can be in helping players achieve a desired result, even when the individual has all but given up. The play is named after the Hail Mary prayer, a traditional Catholic prayer that asks the Virgin Mary to help the person offering the prayer.

A Hail Mary pass occurs when desperate circumstances lead a quarterback to send off a long pass that has little chance of being caught. Somehow, that pass is miraculously caught and allows a team to make a dramatic comeback. Most experts believe its success comes from the quarterback subconsciously invoking a well-practiced motor learning program.

The first known Hail Mary pass occurred on December 28, 1975, when Dallas Cowboys quarterback Roger Staubach was knocked down but still managed to launch a 50-yard (45.7 m) pass to wide receiver Drew Pearson in a game against the Minnesota Vikings. With seconds left in the game, the score was Vikings 14, Cowboys 10. Pearson caught the ball and made a touchdown. After the game, Staubach, a Catholic, stated, "I got knocked down on the play. . . . I closed my eyes and said a Hail Mary."

Quoted in ABC30 Action News, "Here's the History of the NFL's 'Hail Mary' Pass on Its 41st Anniversary," December 28, 2016. https://abc30.com.

then] I'll look at the game like I always do . . . look at the video from it, and do everything I can to compartmentalize what happened this evening, and move on from it in a positive way."[22]

Imagery

Another skill that bolsters athletes' mental toughness and enhances performance is imagery. It is sometimes called visualization, but many experts point out that this term is misleading because all the senses, not just vision, are involved. Studies show that virtually all successful people use some form of imagery, in which an individual imagines that he or she is correctly performing a particular action or skill before executing it during a practice or game. Some football teams, such as the Seattle Seahawks, practice imagery as a group during training camp. According to mental toughness trainer Craig Sigl, "If I had to name one thing that separates elite athletes from lower level athletes, [imagery] is it."[23]

> **imagery**
> A technique in which an individual imagines him- or herself performing a skill correctly, using one or more sensory qualities

Psychologists say imagery is effective because it activates the same areas of the brain that become active when the person actually performs the skill. The most effective way of using imagery, many psychologists state, is to focus on imagining each element of a skill separately before imagining the entire sequence. However, the precise ways in which athletes use imagery vary in different people.

Former NFL kicker Jim Breech credits imagery with helping him cope in high-pressure situations, such as having to kick a 50-yard (45.7 m) field goal with twenty seconds remaining in a game. His imagery process began with creating a mental picture of a third goalpost between the two real goalposts on the football field. He mentally placed the imaginary goalpost at the location he wanted his kick to end up, after he mentally accounted for current wind conditions. "I would see this in my mind's eye, and I'd move it a little to compensate for the wind,"[24] he explains.

41

The imaginary goalpost's position would therefore change every time he imagined it. He found that concentrating on the imaginary goalpost made him forget about coaches, fans, television cameras, and other distractions. He knew he was ready to kick a field goal when nothing else intruded on his thoughts.

The Power of the Mind

Players in all positions need mental qualities such as motivation, self-confidence, and focus. But some positions require certain mental attributes more than other positions do. For example, quarterbacks need the ability to lead and inspire teammates. The Saints' Drew Brees is one NFL quarterback who is widely ac-

Although New Orleans Saints quarterback Drew Brees was named the all-time passing leader in 2018, he's even better known for his mental toughness and ability to lead and inspire his teammates.

claimed as being outstanding in those respects. In October 2018 Brees was named the all-time NFL passing leader, with nearly 72,000 passing yards during his career. But his teammates and others who know him say this achievement pales in comparison to his ability to lead and inspire. "The wonder of Brees has nothing to do with his accumulation of unreal numbers in a pass-happy era," writes Matthew Freedman, an editor for the Action Network website. "The wonder of Brees is that for 17 years he has helped great players become Hall of Famers, good players become great and mediocre players become good. . . . He's made a career of making his teammates the best they can be."[25] Without the mental strength that drives elite players to excel and overcome roadblocks, Brees and others like him would never reach or retain their elite status.

CHAPTER FOUR

Science and Football Equipment

The scientific principles that govern the motion of football players also govern the ways in which the tools of the trade—the football, football field, and protective gear—operate. This equipment and the playing environment are designed to allow players to do the things the sport calls for—running, passing, kicking, and tackling.

The Football

The football's shape, known as a prolate spheroid, is ideal for passing, kicking, and ball carrying. It is important for players to understand how the ball behaves when it is dispatched in these ways so they can use it optimally. Players who know where the ball will be after it descends from the sky and/or bounces have the best chance of recovering it before an opponent does.

When a football bounces, unlike a round ball, its upward motion does not mirror its downward motion. "When it hits the ground, it goes Kerflooey with an out-of-control bounce," writes *Chicago Tribune* reporter Sandy Bauers, who also describes a football as "the klutz of all sports equipment."[26] Newton's third law explains that the bounce behavior of a round ball occurs because the ground reaction force mirrors the force the ball exerts on the ground. But the shape of a football means the direction and distance of its bounce depend on which part of

> **prolate spheroid**
> The shape of a football

the ball hits the ground first, the speed and angle of the hit, and whether the ball is spinning.

However, knowledge of these details does not make the football's bounce behavior predictable. This is why many coaches teach players to simply pounce on and cover a bouncing football rather than watching it bounce to an improved field position. Indeed, failing to promptly pounce on the ball can have costly repercussions, as demonstrated in an October 2018 game between Rutgers University and the University of Maryland. A Maryland kickoff landed on Rutgers's 19-yard-line, and while the Rutgers players watched the ball bounce, the Maryland kickoff squad arrived in time for linebacker Chance Campbell to catch it as it bounced upward. Maryland used its excellent field position to make a field goal.

Up, Up, and Away

A football's airborne behavior is more predictable than its bounce behavior. The goal with many passes and kicks is to maximize the ball's hang time, or the time it stays in the air, and range, or how far it flies. Both the hang time and range depend on the angle and speed at which the ball is launched.

When a quarterback throws a pass, the football follows a path, or trajectory, shaped like an upside-down U, or parabola. First it goes upward due to a force called the lift force. The spin a quarterback puts on the football causes air above it to move slower than the air below it. And according to Bernoulli's principle, put forth by the Swiss scientist and mathematician Daniel Bernoulli in 1738, a fluid, which physicists consider air to be, that is moving slowly creates more pressure than a fast-moving fluid does. Therefore, the greater pressure below the football, where the airflow is slowed down, forces the ball in the direction of the low-pressure area at the top. This lift force opposes the force of gravity that pulls the ball downward, and it contributes to the football's hang time.

parabola
The upside-down U shape of the path an airborne football follows

Projectile Motion and the Quarterback Pass

An understanding of projectile motion helps quarterbacks throw more accurate passes. When the football (or projectile) is thrown, it travels along a path called a parabola. That motion is influenced first by range. Range refers to how far the ball travels once it is thrown. Range, in turn, depends on three factors. The first of these is initial speed, or how fast the ball moves once the quarterback releases it. A harder throw means a higher initial speed. Next is launch angle. This refers to the angle of the ball relative to the ground once it is thrown. A ball that is thrown straight up in the air has a launch angle of 90 degrees. A ball that is thrown directly ahead in a straight line has a launch angle of 0 degrees. The final factor that influences range is initial height. Initial height is the distance between the ball and the ground once the quarterback releases the ball.

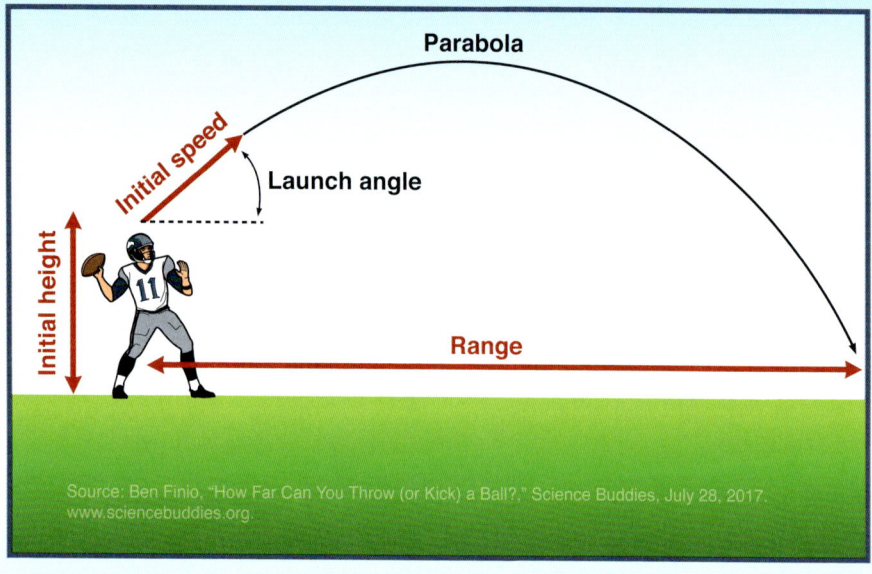

Source: Ben Finio, "How Far Can You Throw (or Kick) a Ball?," Science Buddies, July 28, 2017. www.sciencebuddies.org.

The launch angle of a pass also influences hang time. According to physicist Louis Bloomfield, "If you choose a short bullet pass, you aim the ball almost horizontally so it travels quickly during its brief flight. If you choose a long bomb, you aim about 45 degrees above horizontal so the football arcs high and long."[27] However, since a football does not have any mechanism to keep it moving forward, gravity soon wins the battle with the lift force. The longest hang time for a pass is only four seconds—unless Aaron Rodgers happens to throw a Hail Mary.

In 2016 he did so four times, completing three and making him the new so-called King of Hail Marys. Rodgers sends his Hail Marys higher than those thrown by other NFL quarterbacks; his teammates characterize them as a cross between a pass and a punt. Their hang time has been clocked at 4.35 to 4.4 seconds. Rodgers admits that the increased hang time and the rest of his Hail Mary technique grew out of a conversation he had with former astronaut Mark Kelly. He and Kelly talked about how the height and trajectory of a football depend on the launch angle, wind speed and direction, and air temperature. As Kelly told *Sports Illustrated*, "His Hail Mary passes are like a spaceship re-entering orbit."[28]

Poetry in Motion

Quarterbacks add another force—angular momentum—to the ball by making it spin, or spiral. Like linear momentum, angular momentum is a measurement of an object's motion. However, instead of measuring the object's motion in a straight line, angular momentum quantifies its rotation around a central point or line known as its axis of rotation.

Football players, coaches, and fans often use the phrase "poetry in motion" to describe a perfectly thrown spiral that drops right into a receiver's outstretched hands. However, quarterbacks do not add rotation to make the ball look pretty. "For all its aesthetic beauty, the real payoff of a spiral is its remarkable accuracy,"[29] state journalist Allen St. John and mechanical engineering professor Ainissa G. Ramirez in their book, *Newton's Football*. Quarterbacks achieve accuracy by adding a consistent amount of spin that puts the football on a stable, predictable path with the same nose-first orientation it had when it was launched. This stability occurs because a spiraling football has both linear and angular momentum. According to Newton's first law, the more momentum an object has, the more it resists forces like gravity that act to change its motion.

Kicking the Football

Kicked footballs follow the same principles of physics and biomechanics that passes do. Professional and collegiate teams generally have two types of kickers. Placekickers kick field goals and after-touchdown extra point conversions, and punters usually kick punts and kickoffs. The techniques differ for different types of kicks. Placekickers run up to the ball, which sits in a tee on the ground

This collegiate punter attempts to achieve maximum hang time and range so that his teammates can run downfield. Kicked footballs follow the same scientific principles that passes do.

or is held by a teammate called a ball holder. Punters drop the ball and kick it on its way down, after the center hikes it to them.

The goal for punts and kickoffs is to achieve maximum hang time and range so the kicker's teammates can run downfield to tackle whoever picks up the ball. To achieve this, modern kickers use what is called a soccer-style kick.

In the nineteenth and early twentieth centuries, kickers kicked the football straight on with their toes, mostly using the big toe. During the 1950s several kickers began using soccer-style kicks in which they approached and kicked the ball from the side, using the inside of the foot. Fred Bednarski was the first player to introduce soccer-style kicks to American football in 1953, though many historians credit brothers Pete and Charlie Gogolak, who moved from Hungary to New York with their family in 1956, with this game changer.

The Sidewinder Kicker

Twelve-year-old Zdzislaw Bednarski became Fred Bednarski when his family moved to Texas in 1948, after being liberated from a Nazi concentration camp in 1945. When he started playing American football in junior high school, soccer-style kicks allowed him to send kickoffs into the end zone and to make 50-yard (45.7 m) field goals during his high school and college years. A football scout who saw him kick for the University of Texas expressed amazement about how Bednarski used "the side of his shoe like a sidewinder!"[30] Kicking this way sends the ball farther than kicking it straight on because more of the foot contacts the ball. This greater mass imparts more force, as per Newton's second law. The sideways motion also makes the kicker's hip rotate, adding angular momentum that is transferred to the football.

Coaches and players were initially confused and uncertain about this new kicking innovation. When Bednarski kicked the first-ever soccer-style field goal in collegiate football history during a 1957 game between the University of Texas and the University of Arkansas, confused Arkansas players yelled, "Trick play!

Watch for the fake!"[31] when Bednarski took three steps to the side of the football before kicking a 40-yard (36.6 m) field goal on a fourth down. But soccer-style kicks gradually replaced the older type during the 1960s. This revolutionized football by making field goals an important part of the sport. Before NFL kickers used the new technique, they kicked only one or two field goals per season. In 2018 NFL teams attempted seventeen to forty-two field goals and completed twelve to thirty-seven.

Carrying the Football

Footballs are also designed for carrying. The shape allows ball carriers to tuck the ball between the arm and rib cage while running or being tackled. This makes it difficult for opponents to employ linear or rotational force to push, punch, pry, grab, or knock the ball away from the ball carrier so he fumbles. Most ball carriers use five body areas—the fingers, forearm, rib cage, bicep muscle, and elbow joint—to stabilize and protect the football. The idea is for the entire front tip of the ball to be covered by the fingers or palm, while the wrist, forearm, elbow joint, and rib cage create a pocket in which the ball can be protected. If an opponent tries to dislodge the ball by applying torque to the ball carrier's rib cage, for example, the ball carrier can counteract this by tightening the grip of his fingers on the ball or pressing the ball more snugly between his forearm and rib cage.

In 2016 several NFL and collegiate teams began testing a new high-tech football that beeps when players carry it properly. Coaches and players say the devices have improved players' ability to hang on to the ball. "If I had that ball in high school, I don't think I would've had a fumble," states Washington Redskins running back Matt Jones. "It's teaching me how to squeeze the ball at the point of contact."[32]

The Football Field

The football field is another element of the sport that influences players' motions, decisions, and ability to play the game. Some qualities

The Kicker's Dilemma

Kickers face what is called the kicker's dilemma. Physics professor Peter J. Brancazio says this arises because studies show that kicking at a 40- to 45-degree angle maximizes range, while kicking at a 90-degree angle maximizes hang time. The range for a ball kicked at a 90-degree angle—straight upward—is zero because it goes up and drops straight down, but the hang time increases from about 4 seconds to 6.2 seconds. Most kickers compromise by maximizing either range or hang time.

"Launching a punt at a 55° angle instead of 45°, a punter sacrifices about five yards of distance in exchange for an extra 0.55 seconds of hang time," explains Brancazio. Most punters launch at a 60-degree angle to maximize hang time. Conversely, hang time is not critical for field goals, so placekickers maximize distance using a 43- to 45-degree angle.

Los Angeles Rams punter Johnny Hekker manages to maximize both range and hang time. This makes him "a tremendous weapon," says New England Patriots coach Bill Belichick. Hekker routinely sends punts flying nearly 80 yards (73.2 m) with hang times of about five seconds. This gives the opposing team poor field position on its next drive, and Hekker further confounds them with his Aussie-style kicking technique. It involves dropping the ball straight down with its nose pointing downward before kicking it, instead of parallel to the ground like most punters do. This makes the ball bounce backward when it lands, resulting in an even worse field position for the opponent.

Peter J. Brancazio, "The Physics of Kicking a Football," *Physics Teacher*, October 1985. http://docplayer.net.

Quoted in Dom Cosentino, "Johnny Hekker Is the Punter Every Punter Wants to Be," Deadspin, December 9, 2016. https://deadspin.com.

---

of the field differ for players at different levels of competition. For instance, the size of the area between the goalposts is greater for high school teams than for collegiate and professional teams because more experienced kickers tend to kick more accurately.

The standard football field is 120 yards (109.7 m) long and 53.33 yards (48.8 m) wide. This includes the end zones—the

10 yards (9.1 m) at each end of the field that must be reached to score touchdowns. The field is marked with yard lines every 5 yards (4.6 m), and the numbers corresponding to the yard lines appear every 10 yards (9.1 m). Hash marks appear every 1 yard (91.4 cm). Before hash marks were implemented in 1933, referees placed the ball at the spot where it ended up during the previous play. If this was near a sideline, it limited the plays that could be chosen to those that involved passing or running toward midfield. Placing the ball on or near hash marks in the center of the field opened up more opportunities for plays that used the whole field.

The numbers, yard lines, and hash marks serve as reference points for players, referees, and spectators. A tight end, for example, who knows he will catch a pass at the 20-yard line can use the numbers and lines to gauge his current and intended positions. Numbers and hash marks also help referees assess penalties and determine whether a team has achieved a first down by moving the ball at least 10 yards (9.1 m).

Grass Versus Turf

The lines, numbers, and hash marks on the field are painted on either natural grass or artificial turf. Originally, all football fields contained natural grass. But after the first indoor domed stadiums were built during the 1960s, indoor fields, as well as some outdoor ones, began using artificial turf. Early types of turf, such as Astroturf, were made of fibers and plastics. Many people thought they would cost less than grass, be easier to maintain, and reduce players' injuries because of a uniform consistency that would eliminate tripping on mounds of thick grass or dirt. However, early forms of turf actually led to increases in injuries. Many players complained because wet turf is more slippery than wet grass, and dry turf creates extra friction and holds on to cleats, making it difficult to quickly change direction. Players also said they got bad scrapes from turf fibers ripping up their arms when they were tackled.

Newer forms of artificial turf like FieldTurf contain more grass-like fibers and have padding made of sand and rubber, so the number of turf-related injuries has dropped. However, some studies find that turf-related injuries are still more common than grass-related injuries, while other studies show the opposite. Despite the mixed findings, most professional and many collegiate fields now contain FieldTurf.

Helmets and Pads

Other equipment that is important in football is protective gear such as helmets and pads. By widening the area and lengthening the time for which the force and pressure are applied, the protective gear absorbs part of any force or pressure that impact an individual. According to Newton's second law, this reduces the acceleration and redistributes the mass, thereby reducing the force.

Early football helmets and shoulder pads introduced in the late nineteenth century were made of leather and did little to protect

Early football helmets and pads (pictured is an NFL game in 1950) did not adequately protect players. However, today's equipment is much more sophisticated and contains materials that help absorb the force generated by collisions.

players. Modern helmets, which come with attached face masks, and pads are more effective because they contain materials like viscoelastic foam. The National Aeronautics and Space Administration invented viscoelastic foam to protect astronauts from g-forces that impact them during space travel. The foam crumples on impact like car bumpers do and quickly returns to its original shape after it absorbs the forces generated by the impact.

G-forces are a measurement of how much the acceleration in an activity such as violently colliding with an opponent affects the people involved. One g is the acceleration due to the normal

The Deflategate Scandal

The pressure inside a football is one factor that affects its behavior and interactions with players. Pressure depends on the amount of air pumped into the ball and is caused by the force of air molecules hitting the inside surface of the ball. The importance of pressure is illustrated by a scandal known as Deflategate, which began during a play-off game on January 3, 2015, after quarterback Tom Brady and two other New England Patriots employees were accused of purposely deflating game balls. A ball with less pressure is easier to hold, throw, and catch. NFL rules mandate that game footballs be inflated to about 13 pounds (5.9 kg) of air per square inch (psi), but these balls tested about 2 psi low when equipment managers performed routine pressure tests. Several players on the opposing team, the Colts, also reported that when they intercepted a couple of Brady's passes, the footballs felt unusually soft.

After an investigation, the NFL suspended Brady for four games and fined the Patriots $1 million, but Brady appealed this decision in court with help from professors of engineering and physics, who noted that footballs naturally deflate somewhat when they are moved from the warm environment of the locker room to the cold outdoors. On the other hand, physicists and engineers working for the NFL stated that the only scientific explanation for the lower pressure was that someone deliberately released air from the footballs. In the end, no one was sure what really happened.

force of gravity that drives objects downward. Its value is 32.15 feet (9.8 m) per second. People riding on a roller coaster experience forces of about 5 g's, and pilots in F-16 fighter jets experience about 9 g's. Scientists have measured the forces on colliding football players to be as high as 150 g's.

However, the number and severity of injuries, particularly brain injuries, increased after effective protection became available. Medical experts say this happened because of what is known as compensatory behavior. This is a tendency for people to rely on protective gear for safety and to therefore stop behaving cautiously. "If you wear safety equipment, you're inclined to take greater risk,"[33] explains neurologist Harry Kerasidis. This does not just happen in football; studies show that bicyclists who wear helmets and drivers who wear seat belts tend to drive faster than those who do not. Thus, protective gear does not necessarily make a sport or other pastime safer.

> **compensatory behavior**
> The tendency for people who wear safety equipment to take unwise chances because they are relying on the equipment for protection

Spectators usually focus on football players and footballs when they watch competitive football games. However, other tools of the trade, such as the field and the various parts of players' uniforms, are equally important in determining the outcome and safety of the sport.

CHAPTER FIVE

Football Injuries

Tackle football at all levels of competition leads to injuries to many parts of the body. In fact, a 2016 study by sports medicine doctor David W. Lawrence and his colleagues at the University of Toronto noted that "football has one of the highest rates of all-cause injury, including concussion, of all major sports."[34] Most injuries result from collisions between offensive and defensive players and collisions in which an opponent slams a player to the ground. The type and severity of the injuries depend on the composition of the field and on the size, speed, momentum, strength, and protective gear of the players.

concussion
A traumatic brain injury from a hit to the head that leads to a temporary loss of mental function

A typical NFL game contains one hundred or more violent tackles, and similar practices at other levels of competition make injuries likely. The large size of twenty-first-century players is one factor that underlies the vast number of serious injuries. In 1920 an average professional football lineman weighed 190 pounds (86.2 kg). When the 300-pound (136 kg) William "the Refrigerator" Perry played for the Chicago Bears in the 1980s and early 1990s, he was considered to be unusually massive. But the average lineman during the second decade of the twenty-first century weighed 300 pounds. A fast-moving 300-pound lineman hits an opponent with approximately one-and-a-half times more force than one who weighs 190 pounds.

Head Injuries and Brain Disease

Health experts are concerned about the increasingly forceful impacts in modern-day football games because of increasing awareness of the devastating consequences. Head and neck injuries caused by violent impacts are of most immediate concern because recent studies of the brains of deceased former NFL players indicate that 99 percent show evidence of a degenerative brain disease called chronic traumatic encephalopathy (CTE). Neuroscientist Ann McKee and her colleagues at Boston University, who performed most of these studies, found that these brains contained a buildup of a protein called tau, which is known to underlie brain diseases characterized by dementia, a decline in memory and thinking skills.

Other studies find that CTE results from repeated blows to the head, even those that do not seem serious when they occur. Doctors and the general public once thought that head trauma that did not result in concussion and/or unconsciousness was not serious. Concussion is defined as a traumatic brain injury that leads to temporary changes in mental function. Boston University neurosurgery professor Robert Cantu calls the belief that athletes must experience concussion and/or unconsciousness to develop brain damage "the number-one most serious misconception"[35] among participants in contact sports.

Repeated hits to the head can even lead to CTE in young people. After former New York Giants safety Tyler Sash died from an accidental drug overdose in 2015 at age twenty-seven, McKee found evidence of CTE in parts of his brain that control memory, emotion, and self-control. This damage was consistent with Sash's family's reports that he showed confusion, memory loss, and extreme anger and aggressiveness before he died. "Even though he was only 27, he played 16 years of football, and we're finding over

chronic traumatic encephalopathy (CTE)
Progressive brain damage from repeated blows to the head that affects memory and other mental functions

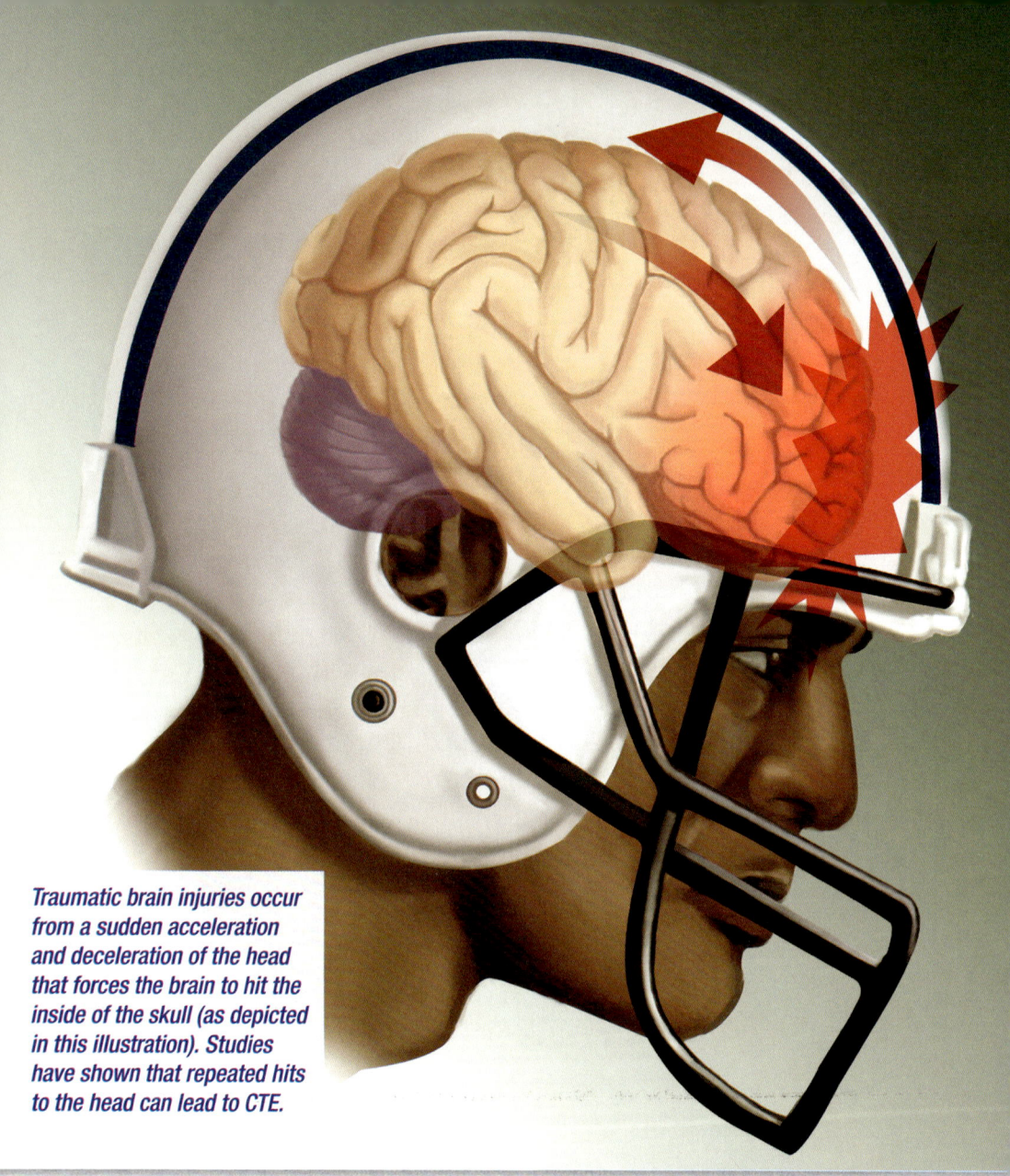

Traumatic brain injuries occur from a sudden acceleration and deceleration of the head that forces the brain to hit the inside of the skull (as depicted in this illustration). Studies have shown that repeated hits to the head can lead to CTE.

and over that it's the duration of exposure to football that gives you a high risk for C.T.E.,"[36] McKee states. Indeed, studies run by McKee and others indicate that athletes who start playing tackle football before age twelve are at highest risk for CTE because their brains do not develop optimally after multiple hits.

Studies at the Virginia Tech Center for Injury Biomechanics found that children as young as age seven who played in Pop

Warner youth football leagues experienced dozens of hits to the head that measured more than 40 g's in a single season. The league changed its rules to prohibit such hits around 2012, and the number of hits to the head fell by 50 percent. Still, controversies about children playing tackle football persist. Some experts believe safer equipment and new rules can mitigate the risks. But Cantu, who is considered one of the foremost authorities on brain injuries, has stated many times, "I don't think parents should bring kids into tackle football short of high school."[37]

In addition, many players and their families believe high school and collegiate coaches should stop encouraging players to play when injured. Some players have filed lawsuits because of tragic results. For example, in 2018 nineteen-year-old Destin Julian filed a lawsuit against his former coach, Gary Lee, at Hamady High School in Michigan for ignoring or disregarding players' injuries. Lee called players who complained "sissies" and told them to "play through the pain."[38] At age sixteen, Julian experienced a violent hit to the head during practice and another during a game that same week. The concussions left him with ongoing pain, seizures, mood swings, and anger-management problems that shattered his dream of playing football at the University of Alabama.

What Causes Brain Injuries?

The cause of traumatic brain injuries is sudden acceleration and deceleration of the head that forces the brain to hit the inside of the skull. Sometimes these forces cause the head and neck to twist. In fact, a 2017 study by biomedical engineers at Stanford University found that the worst damage occurs when nerve fibers become twisted. The researchers noted that the face mask attached to the helmet exacerbates the twisting effect, particularly when an opponent grabs it. No matter the cause, "the brain was not meant to sustain the force caused by athletes crashing head-first into each other,"[39] states neurologist Harry Kerasidis.

Other studies prove that even high-tech helmets do not protect players against these injuries. This is why some health authorities have suggested that players train without helmets. Kinesiologist Erik Swartz at the University of New Hampshire, for example, states that his studies indicate that collegiate football players who train with no helmets experience 30 percent fewer head collisions and injuries. He says he believes this happens because the absence of a helmet triggers motor learning that forces "the instinctive desire to protect their head [to] become muscle memory."[40]

Many head and neck injuries happen when players lower their heads to tackle an opponent or to defend themselves against being tackled. This is referred to as spearing. It is proved to increase the risk of serious head, neck, and spinal cord injuries in part because of the so-called pocketing effect. This happens when spearing compresses an opponent's shoulder pads and creates a pocket that traps the spearer's head, thereby increasing the amount of time for which these compressive forces act.

spearing
Colliding with an opponent with the head tucked so the top of the head rams into the opponent's torso

Increased awareness of the seriousness of head injuries led the NFL and other football leagues to adopt new rules that prohibit spearing and require doctors to immediately evaluate and bench players with symptoms of head injuries. However, spearing still occurs. The most egregious offenses occur when NFL players deliberately do illegal things to force star players out of a game. In December 2017, for example, Thomas Davis of the Carolina Panthers did an illegal helmet-to-helmet hit on the Packers' star receiver, Davante Adams, causing Adams to miss the rest of the game because of a concussion. Referees imposed a 15-yard (13.7 m) penalty on the Panthers, and the NFL suspended Davis for two games. But as former NFL quarterback and present-day NFL analyst David Carr noted, "The Carolina

Tragic Injuries Lead to Change

Sometimes it takes tragic injuries or deaths to motivate football rule changes. One such injury occurred in 1978, when the Patriots' Darryl Stingley became a quadriplegic after the Raiders' Jack Tatum viciously slammed him to the ground. At the time, this was legal. Tatum and the Raiders were, in fact, known for their extreme violence on the field, and Tatum took pride in his nickname of the Assassin. In his book *Call Me Assassin*, he wrote that he fully intended to deliver "an intimidating hit" to Stingley, even though Stingley had already missed catching the ball. He also wrote, "I like to believe that my best hits border on felonious assault." The NFL changed its rules to prohibit overly violent hits and tackles after Stingley's injury.

Another rule change occurred in 2001, after Minnesota Vikings offensive tackle Korey Stringer died from heatstroke at a summer training camp. Stringer's body temperature was 108°F (42.2°C) when he arrived at a hospital and died of organ failure. A temperature of 104°F (40°C) or higher can be fatal. NFL policies changed to require teams to allow players to practice in lightweight, light-colored uniforms in hot weather, to provide shade and water at all times, and to require the presence of a team doctor and an ambulance at all practices and games.

Quoted in Peter Richmond, "Grace After the Fall," *New York Times*, December 30, 2007. www.nytimes.com.

Panthers were able to eliminate Adams, who had been the Packers' most productive receiver over the past six weeks, and all it took was a 15-yard penalty."[41] The Panthers won the game.

Other Injuries

Collisions and other factors are responsible for injuries to parts of the body besides the head. One of the most tragic injuries occurred on August 12, 1978, when Oakland Raiders defensive back Jack Tatum hit Patriots receiver Darryl Stingley in the neck and slammed him to the ground after Stingley jumped to catch a pass. The hit fractured Stingley's fourth and fifth cervical vertebrae in his spine and left him permanently paralyzed from the neck down.

In 2017 Aaron Rodgers broke his collarbone when Minnesota Vikings linebacker Anthony Barr sacked him and fell on Rodgers's shoulder. Similar injuries to other quarterbacks led the NFL to change its so-called roughing the passer rule in 2018. Defensive players can no longer land on a quarterback with all or most of their body weight. The rule has been criticized by players and coaches who believe the difficulty of tackling and not falling on a quarterback will lead to injuries. This concern materialized in September 2018 when Miami Dolphins defensive lineman William Hayes tore the anterior cruciate ligament (ACL) in his knee while trying to avoid falling on Oakland Raiders quarterback Derek Carr. This sidelined Hayes for the rest of the season. Carr, among others, blamed the new rule, stating,

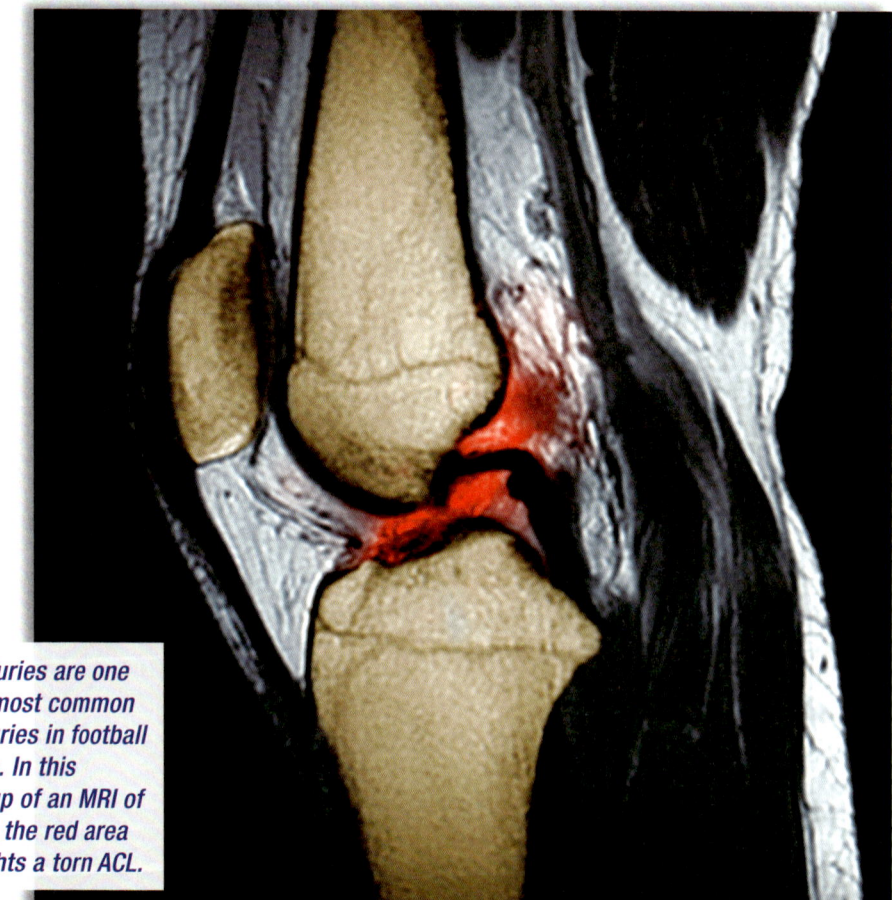

ACL injuries are one of the most common leg injuries in football players. In this close-up of an MRI of a knee, the red area highlights a torn ACL.

"I wish the guy would have just landed on me instead of tearing his ACL . . . nobody wants that."[42]

ACL injuries are one of the most common leg injuries in football players. The ACL is responsible for stabilizing the knee joint. A 2018 study by exercise science professor Craig E. Pfeifer and his colleagues at Lander University found that more than 70 percent of ACL injuries in football players occur during sudden changes of direction. Friction between the person's shoes and the turf or grass beneath his feet, coupled with the torque exerted by the sudden motion, overextend the ACL and lead to full or partial tearing.

Treatment for severe ACL tears usually includes surgery and rehabilitation that lasts six to twelve months. Some football players can resume playing after such surgery and rehabilitation; in 2017, for example, Baltimore Ravens cornerback Tavon Young missed an entire season after surgery to repair an ACL tear but recovered well enough to continue playing pro football. Modern surgical techniques have increased the chances that players can return to a football career, but a 2016 study by scientists at Thomas Jefferson University found that 21 percent to 37 percent of NFL players who sustain one or more ACL injuries never recover enough to resume playing professional football.

Back injuries are also common in football players. Sometimes these result from collisions with opponents and/or the ground, but other times they are caused by players engaging in overly strenuous training exercises or movements during games. J.J. Watt, for instance, engaged in lifting and manipulating heavy weights during the off-season and in between games. In fact, his off-season practice of flipping 1,000-pound (453.6 kg) truck tires became widely known. But his strenuous workouts led to a serious back injury in September 2016 that required surgery and left him unable to play for the remainder of the season. During his recovery and afterward, his personal trainer taught him to do exercises that rebuilt strength and power in his entire body without overstraining muscles and other body parts.

Another common injury—to the rotator cuff in the shoulder—can be caused by a collision or by overuse of the shoulder. The rotator cuff is a group of muscles and tendons that stabilize the shoulder joint. It is most likely to tear in athletes like baseball pitchers and quarterbacks who subject it to large amounts of rotational force. In one well-publicized career-ending injury, quarterback Greg Cook of the Cincinnati Bengals tore his rotator cuff when an opposing linebacker fell on his shoulder in 1969. Cook, who was acclaimed as the best-ever quarterback, had to retire at age twenty-seven because of the injury.

The Dangers of Heat

Besides the many types of injuries that affect football players, heat-related dehydration, heat exhaustion, and potentially fatal heatstroke, in which the body temperature rises to dangerous levels, are ongoing dangers, particularly during the practices, training camps, and preseason games that start in the late summer months. After Vikings tackle Korey Stringer died from heatstroke in 2001, increased awareness led to new rules about drink, shade, and emergency treatment availability.

Still, each year several heat-related deaths occur among high school, collegiate, and professional players. After University of Maryland offensive lineman Jordan McNair died of heatstroke in June 2018, head coach DJ Durkin was fired after an investigation into the culture of fear and intimidation he established. Investigators determined that McNair died because Durkin's staff failed to treat him or call emergency responders until it was too late.

Football and Injury

The many serious injuries and other health problems that result from football concern players, families, and medical professionals not only because they often mean a player, particularly a profes-

Bootin' Ben Kicks Injury Goodbye

Some football players adapt to physical limitations imposed by an injury so they can continue to play the sport they love. In 1941, for example, University of New Mexico kicker Ben Agajanian had four toes on his kicking foot amputated after they were crushed in a freight elevator accident at the Coca-Cola bottling plant where he worked part time. Doctors told him he would never play football again, but Agajanian asked his surgeons to square off the remaining part of his foot so he could continue to kick.

After healing, Agajanian tried to kick a football, but it was extremely painful, and his shoe filled with blood. However, a shoemaker made him a special squared-off leather boot that helped him kick faster, farther, and more accurately than ever. As per Newton's second law, the greater mass of the boot's toe area applied greater force to the football.

Agajanian set kicking records working with ten professional football teams for seventeen years. He became known as Bootin' Ben and is widely known for pioneering the Agajanian two-step, a modified soccer-style kick in which a kicker takes three steps backward and two to the side before connecting with the football. After retiring from kicking, he worked for twenty years as the first-ever kicking coach for the Dallas Cowboys. He also established a kicking clinic and camp in Long Beach, California, where he trained hundreds of kickers of all ages.

sional player, must retire, but also because the chances of life long problems such as CTE are high. And for some, a serious football injury abruptly turns the life of a highly trained athlete into one that involves dealing with devastating disabilities. This has immense physical, psychological, and emotional effects. Some players never accept their situation, while others manage to re-invent themselves. Some begin new lives as coaches or sports media commentators. Others become teachers or writers. Darryl Stingley was one former NFL player who was initially bitter about the tackle that paralyzed him, but he learned to accept his fate and to be thankful to be alive. He aggressively worked out to strengthen his body, got a college education, drove himself around in a specially equipped van, and inspired countless people with his positive attitude until his death in 2007. In 1983 Stingley wrote an article for *Ebony* magazine in which he stated, "I can help people do more, do more for people, in my present condition than I could when I was a football player. When I'm gone, when He calls me, I'd like to be remembered not as the football player who had an accident, but as a man who made a great contribution to his fellow man."[43]

Despite the ever-present risk of injury, football remains one of the most popular sports in America. Although many people,

A player breaks a tackle during a youth league football game. Despite its risks, football remains one of America's most popular sports.

including sports doctors, trainers, coaches, and safety device manufacturers, remain committed to making the sport safer, the very nature of football makes it unlikely that it will lose its place as a risky sport. As sports medicine specialists William N. Levine and Brett D. Owens write in an article on the American Orthopaedic Society for Sports Medicine website, "Injuries occur during football games and practice due to the combination of high speeds and full contact. . . . The force applied to either bringing an opponent to the ground or resisting being brought to the ground makes football players prone to injury anywhere on their bodies, regardless of protective equipment."[44]

SOURCE NOTES

Introduction: Science Affects Everything About Football

1. Quoted in Matt Vensel, "The Strongest Arm: Experts Break Down Joe Flacco's Powerful Delivery," *Baltimore Sun*, June 29, 2013. http://articles.baltimoresun.com.

Chapter One: Physics and Football

2. Quoted in NBC Learn, "Science of NFL Football: Newton's First Law of Motion," October 1, 2010. www.nbclearn.com.
3. Chad Orzel, "Football Physics: The Forces Behind Those Big Hits," *Forbes*, October 11, 2015. www.forbes.com.
4. Chris B. Brown, "NFL Strategy: Darren Sproles and the Rise of the Space Player," Grantland, October 11, 2011. http://grantland.com.

Chapter Two: Biomechanics and Football

5. Quoted in David Fleming, "The Pursuit of Throwing Perfectly," ESPN, April 21, 2010. www.espn.com.
6. Quoted in Phil Perry, "After Practices, Patriots Head to the Hills," NBC Sports, July 27, 2016. www.nbcsports.com.
7. Kevin Clark, "The Reason the Patriots Always Come Back," Ringer, January 30, 2018. www.theringer.com.
8. Mark Bullock, "How the Rams' Aaron Donald Is a Complete Game-Wrecker for NFL Offenses," *Washington Post*, August 31, 2018. www.washingtonpost.com.
9. Quoted in Stack, "Offensive Line Training with the Houston Texans' 'Tanks.'" www.stack.com.

Chapter Three: Mind Matters

10. Quoted in Oliver Thomas, "What Tom Brady's Peers Have Said over the Last Five Years of NFL 'Top 100' Rankings," Pats Pulpit, June 27, 2018. www.patspulpit.com.

11. Quoted in Jeremy Koenigs, "Mason City Graduate Carlisle Teaches Strength in Football, Life with Seattle Seahawks," *Mason City (IA) Globe Gazette*, December 5, 2015. https://globegazette.com.
12. Quoted in Gary D'Amato, "Packers-Cowboys 1967 NFL Championship Game," *Milwaukee Journal Sentinel*, December 28, 2017. www.jsonline.com.
13. Quoted in D'Amato, "Packers-Cowboys 1967 NFL Championship Game."
14. Travis Brody, "10 Ways to Become a Better Football Player," *Growth of a Game* (blog), November 1, 2014. www.growthofagame.com.
15. Quoted in Ron Clements, "Brett Favre Recalls Trash-Talking Rivalry with 'Crazy' Warren Sapp," Sporting News, August 7, 2016. www.sportingnews.com.
16. Quoted in Jim Corbett, "The Art of Smack: Some of the Best Ever Trash Talkers Share Their Tricks," *USA Today*, January 27, 2014. www.usatoday.com.
17. Nick Mordowanec, "Michigan State Football: Spartans Stun Notre Dame on Trick Play in Overtime," Bleacher Report, September 19, 2010. https://bleacherreport.com.
18. Quoted in Philip Sikes, "Virtual Reality," Clemson Tigers, November 21, 2015. https://clemsontigers.com.
19. Anne M. Graybiel and Scott T. Grafton, "The Striatum: Where Skills and Habits Meet," *Cold Spring Harbor Perspectives in Biology*, August 7, 2015. www.ncbi.nlm.nih.gov.
20. Mike Edger, "Resilience and Overcoming Performance Errors," Sport Psychology Today, July 11, 2014. www.sportpsychologytoday.com.
21. Childs Walker, "Ravens Lose to Saints on the Unthinkable Play, a Missed Extra Point by Justin Tucker," *Baltimore Sun*, October 21, 2018. www.baltimoresun.com.
22. Quoted in Walker, "Ravens Lose to Saints on the Unthinkable Play, a Missed Extra Point by Justin Tucker."
23. Craig Sigl, "How (and Why) to Do Visualization for Football," *USA Football Blog*, October 13, 2014. https://blogs.usafootball.com.

24. Quoted in Allen St. John and Ainissa G. Ramirez, *Newton's Football*. New York: Ballantine, 2013, p. 67.
25. Matthew Freedman, "Drew Brees' Record-Breaking Career: His Journey to Becoming NFL's All-Time Passing Leader," Action Network, October 9, 2018. www.actionnetwork.com.

Chapter Four: Science and Football Equipment

26. Sandy Bauers, "Psst! Pass It On: Quarterbacks' Big Secret in the Spiral," *Chicago Tribune*, November 20, 1994. www.chicagotribune.com.
27. Louis Bloomfield, "The Science of Football," *Washington Post*, October 13, 1999. www.washingtonpost.com.
28. Quoted in Greg Bishop, "The Art of the Hail Mary: Why Rodgers Is So Successful with NFL's Most Improbable Play," *Sports Illustrated*, January 13, 2017. www.si.com.
29. St. John and Ramirez, *Newton's Football*, p. 10.
30. Quoted in Jon Dasilva, "The Fred Bednarski Story," Texas Legacy Support Network. www.texas.lsn.org.
31. Quoted in Dasilva, "The Fred Bednarski Story."
32. Quoted in Associated Press, "NFL Teams Hoping to Reduce Fumbles with Beeping Footballs," *USA Today*, June 21, 2016. www.usatoday.com.
33. Harry Kerasidis, "Sports Concussion Psychology: Should Helmets Be Taken Off?," *Psychology Today*, June 4, 2014. www.psychologytoday.com.

Chapter Five: Football Injuries

34. David W. Lawrence et al., "Influence of Extrinsic Risk Factors on National Football League Injury Rates," *Orthopaedic Journal of Sports Medicine*, March 31, 2016. http://journals.sagepub.com.
35. Quoted in Sports Letter, "SL Interview: Dr. Robert Cantu Speaks Out About Concussions in Youth Sports," LA84 Foundation, October 1, 2012. https://la84.org.

36. Quoted in Bill Pennington, "C.T.E. Is Found in an Ex-Giant Tyler Sash, Who Died at 27," *New York Times*, January 26, 2016. www.nytimes.com.
37. Quoted in Sports Letter, "SL Interview."
38. Quoted in Joshua Rhett Miller, "Football Coach Urged 'Sissy' Players to Play Hurt: Suit," *New York Post*, March 6, 2018. https://nypost.com.
39. Kerasidis, "Sports Concussion Psychology."
40. Quoted in Stephanie Pappas, "Can Football Ever Be Safe?," Live Science, October 6, 2017. www.livescience.com.
41. David Carr, "That Hit on Davante Adams? Here's How the NFL Could Police and Prevent It," *Fresno (CA) Bee*, December 20, 2017. www.fresnobee.com.
42. Quoted in Adam Stites, "The Dolphins Say the NFL's Roughing the Passer Penalty Is to Blame for William Hayes' ACL Tear," SB Nation, September 26, 2018. www.sbnation.com.
43. Darryl Stingley, "Happy to Be Alive," *Ebony*, October 1983, p. 68.
44. William N. Levine and Brett D. Owens, "Preventing Football Injuries," Stop Sports Injuries, American Orthopaedic Society for Sports Medicine, 2017. www.stopsportsinjuries.org.

FOR FURTHER RESEARCH

Books

Nicole Brooks Bethea and Caio Cacau, *The Science of Football with Max Axiom, Super Scientist*. Mankato, MN: Capstone, 2015.

Timothy Gay, *The Physics of Football*. New York: Harper, 2004.

Sean McCollum, *Full STEAM Football: Science, Technology, Engineering, Arts, and Mathematics of the Game*. Mankato, MN: Capstone, 2018.

Jennifer Guess McKerley, *Football*. Farmington Hills, MI: Lucent Books, 2012.

Ryan Nagelhout, *The Science of Football*. New York: PowerKids, 2015.

Gregory Nicolai, *The Science of Football: The Top Ten Ways Science Affects the Game*. Mankato, MN: Capstone, 2016.

Internet Sources

Ryan Basen, "Can Science Solve Football's Concussion Crisis?," NBC News, October 27, 2017. www.nbcnews.com.

Amanda Onion, "The Science Behind Football Tackles," ABC News, January 23, 2018. https://abcnews.go.com.

Chad Orzel, "Football Physics: Why Throw a Spiral?," *Forbes*, October 5, 2015. www.forbes.com.

Chad Orzel, "Football Physics: How Would Changing the Laws of Physics Change Football?," *Forbes*, November 22, 2015. www.forbes.com.

Scientific American, "Introducing the Science of Pro Football," 2010. www.scientificamerican.com.

Websites

American Society of Biomechanics (www.asbweb.org). The American Society of Biomechanics is an organization for professionals who work in the field of biomechanics. The website includes information about academic, industry, and clinical research; products that relate to biomechanics; and the subspecialties that exist in biomechanics, such as how biomechanics underlies sports.

Brain Injury Research Institute (www.protectthebrain.org). The Brain Injury Research Institute is an organization that studies the short- and long-term impact of brain injuries, especially CTE, in athletes and others who sustain frequent brain injuries. A group of doctors founded the organization after discovering CTE in the brain of deceased NFL player Mike Webster in 2002. The website contains information about all aspects of CTE.

ESPN *Sport Science* (www.espn.com). The ESPN *Sport Science* television series explores the science behind a variety of sports, including football. This website allows users to follow links to view videos of specific episodes of the show, including those connected to the science of football.

Live Science (www.livescience.com). Live Science is a website that features news stories about many aspects of science, including sports science. Putting "football science" into the search box on the site generates a list of relevant articles on studies about everything from football safety to nutrition tips for players to the physics of the football itself.

***Science of NFL Football*, National Science Foundation** (www.nsf.gov). This website contains videos and transcripts of a ten-part series in which scientists, NFL players, and reporter Lester Holt explore and explain the science that underlies various aspects of football. Each episode examines a different scientific principle, such as projectile motion, kinematics, or Newton's laws of motion.

Sports Science News, ScienceDaily (www.sciencedaily.com). This website features news articles about various types of scientific research related to the science of sports. Some articles focus on a specific sport; others apply to the science of sports in general.

INDEX

Note: Boldface page numbers indicate illustrations.

acceleration, 9, 11–13
Adams, Davante, 60–61
adenosine triphosphate (ATP), 23, 25
aerodynamic drag, 15
Agajanian, Ben, 65
agility, training for, 29
Alworth, Lance, 6
Amendola, Danny, 26
American Orthopaedic Society for Sports Medicine (website), 67
Anderson, Henry, 13–14
Andrews, David, 8
Andrie, George, 33
angular momentum, 47
anterior cruciate ligament (ACL), 62–63, **63**
Astroturf, 52

Baalke, Trent, 24
back injuries, 63–64
Baltimore Ravens, 4–5
Barr, Anthony, 62
Bass, Tom, 6
Bates, Aaron, 36
Bauers, Sandy, 44
Bednarski, Fred (Zdzislaw), 49–50
Belichick, Bill, 51
Bernoulli, Daniel, 45
biomechanics, defined, 4, 6
Bloomfield, Louis, 46
Bootin' Ben, 65
Bradshaw, Terry, 16
Brady, Tom
  Deflategate and, 54
  mental strength of, 32
  playing in Denver, 25
  plays at Super Bowl 53, 8–9, **10**, 10–11

brain injuries
  causes of, 59–60
  chronic traumatic encephalopathy (CTE), 57–58, **58**
  concussions, 56, 57, 60
Brancazio, Peter J., 51
Breech, Jim, 41–42
Brees, Drew, **42,** 42–43
Brody, Travis, 34–35
Brown, Chris B., 18
Bruschi, Tedy, 25
Buckner, DeForest, 24
Bullock, Mark, 29

Caldwell, Jim, 31
Call Me Assassin (Tatum), 61
calories, 24–25
Campbell, Chance, 45
Cantu, Robert, 57, 59
cardiovascular system, 24
Carlisle, Chris, 32–33
Carolina Panthers, 37, 60–61
Carr, David, 60–61
Carr, Derek, 32, 62–63
Carroll, Pete, 32–33
carrying, 50
center of mass/center of gravity, 16–19
Chicago Tribune (newspaper), 44
chronic traumatic encephalopathy (CTE), 57–58, **58**
Clark, Kevin, 27
Clausen, Jimmy, 20–21
collisions
  as major source of injuries, 56
  third law of motion and, 13–15
compensatory behavior, 55
Compton, Tom, 29
concussions, 56, 57, 60
confidence, 35–36
Conroy, Dan, 36
conservation of energy, law of, 14–15
Cook, Greg, 64

74

Cousins, Kirk, 29

Dallas Cowboys, 6–7, 33
Dantonio, Mark, 35–36
Davis, Thomas, 60
dedication, 34–35
Deflategate, 54
Denver Broncos, 4–5, 25
depression, 37
diet, 24–26
Donald, Aaron, 29, **30**

Ebony (magazine), 65–66
elevation and oxygen, 25
Elflein, Pat, 29
endurance activities and cardiovascular system, 24
energy, 14, 22–23
explosive power, 28

faking out, 35–36
fast-twitch (FT) fibers, 21, 23
Favre, Brett, 35
Fetkovich, John, 16
field
   area between goalposts, 51
   grass versus turf, 52–53
   standard, 51–52
FieldTurf, 52–53
Fitzgerald, Craig, 29–30
Flacco, Joe, 4–5, **5**, 31
focus, 35
football, the
   pressure within, 54
   shape of, 44–45, 50
force
   defined, 5
   lift and, 45
   muscle size and, 27
Fox, John, 25
Francisco 49ers, 5
Franklin-Myers, John, 9
Freedman, Matthew, 43
friction, 15
Fuqua, John, 16

Gantt, Charlie, 36
Garrett, Jason, 6–7

g-forces, 54–55
Gillman, Sid, 6
goalposts, area between, 51
Gogolak, Charlie, 49
Gogolak, Pete, 49
Grabowski, Keith, 33
gravity
   action of, 9, 45
   effects of weaker, 18
   energy and, 10
   overcoming, 3
   weight and, 9
Green Bay Packers, 7, 33
ground reaction force, 9, 13
growth factors, 28
Guerin, Tish, 37

Hail Mary pass, 40, 46–47
Hall, Brandon, 28
hang time
   described, 45
   launch angle and, 45, 46, 51
   longest, 46–47
   speed of throw and, 45
Harrington, Joey, 13
Harris, Franco, 16
Hauschka, Stephen, 13–14
Hayes, Lester, 35
Hayes, William, 62–63
heatstroke, 61, 64
Hekker, Johnny, 51
helmets, **53**, 53–55, 59–60
Henery, Alex, 11
Hermsmeyer, Josh, 26
Hogan, Chris, 10–11

Ice Bowl, 33
imagery skills, 41–42
Immaculate Deception, 16
Immaculate Reception, 15–16
Indianapolis Colts, 54
inertia
   defined, 10
   Newton's first law, 8–9, **10**, 10–11, 47
injuries
   adapting to, 65
   to anterior cruciate ligament (ACL), 62–63, **63**

back, 63–64
heatstroke, 61, 64
major source of, 56
neck and spinal cord, 60, 61–62
number and severity of, 55
protective gear and, 55, 59–60
rate of, 56
rotator cuff, 64
turf and, 52–53
See also brain injuries
inspiration, ability to instill in others, 43

Jaworski, Ron, 5
Jones, Jacoby, 4
Jones, Matt, 50
Julian, Destin, 59

Kelly, Mark, 47
Kerasidis, Harry, 55, 59
kicker's dilemma, 51
kicking and kickers
  Bootin' Ben, 65
  dilemma faced by, 51
  by placekickers, 48–49
  by punters, 48, **48**, 49, 51
  sidewinder, 49–50
kinesiology, defined, 4
kinetic energy
  ATP and, 23, 25
  transformation of potential energy into, 10, 11
King of Hail Marys, 46–47
"king of trash talk," 35

Lane, Chuck, 33
launch angle
  and hang time, 45, 46, **46**, 51
  punts and, 51
Lawrence, David W., 56
Lee, Gary, 59
Levine, William N., 67
lift force, 45, 46
ligaments, 21, 62–63, **63**
light, speed of, 18
linear motion, 8, 47
linemen, training, 29–30, **30**
Little Giants fake out, 35–36
Littleton, Cory, 11

Lombardi, Vince, 7, 33
lubricated friction, 15

Manning, Peyton, **34,** 34–35
mass
  center of, 16–19
  described, 9
  first law of motion and, 11
  friction and, 15
  second law of motion and, 11–12
mathematics and pass patterns, 6–7
McDaniel, Larry, 20
McKee, Ann, 57–58
McNair, Jordan, 64
mental skills
  ability to inspire others, 43
  confidence, 35–36
  dedication, 34–35
  focus, 35
  imagery and, 41–42
  motivation, 32–33
  motor learning and, 36–38, 40
  resilience, 38–41
mental warfare, 35–36
Michigan State University (MSU) Spartans, 35–36
Mile High Miracle, 4–6
Minnesota Vikings, 61, 64
mood disorders, 37
motion
  angular, 47
  linear, 8, 47
  projectile, 45–47, **46**
  rotational, 8
  See also Newton's laws of motion
motivation, 32–33
motor learning, 36–38, 40
musculoskeletal system
  agility and, 29
  energy for muscles, 22–23, 25
  parts of, 21
  passing and, 21–22, **22**
  strengthening, 27–28
myocytes, 21

National Aeronautics and Space Administration, 54
neck injuries, 60, 61–62

New England Patriots, 26–**27,** 54
Newton, Isaac, 8
   See also Newton's laws of motion
Newton, the (pound-force), 9
Newton's Football (St. John and Ramirez), 47
Newton's laws of motion
   first, 8–9, **10,** 10–11, 47
   second, 11–13, 53, 65
   third, 13–16, 44
Notre Dame Fighting Irish, 35–36

Oakland Raiders
   Immaculate Reception and, 15–16
   trash talking to win, 35
   violence on field, 61
Ord, Michael, 16
Orzel, Chad, 14, 18
Owens, Brett D., 67
oxygen
   cardiovascular system and, 24
   elevation and, 25
   energy for muscles and, 22–23

parabola, 45
passing, 6–7, 20–22, **22**
Pearson, Drew, 40
Perry, William "the Refrigerator," 56
Peterson, Adrian, 23
Pfeifer, Craig E., 63
physics, defined, 4, 8
Pittsburgh Steelers, 15–16
placekickers, 48–49
plyometrics, 28
Pop Warner football, 58–59
potential energy
   ATP and, 23
   described, 9–10
   from food, 24
   transformation into kinetic energy, 10, 11, 25
pound-force, 9
projectile motion, 45–47, **46**
prolate spheroid, 44
protective gear, **53,** 53–55, 59–60
psychology, defined, 4
punters, 48, **48,** 49, 51
Pythagorean theorem, 6–7

quickness, training for, 28–29

Ramirez, Ainissa G., 47
range, 45, **46**
reaction time, 36–38
resilience, 38–41
Robey-Coleman, Nickell, 11
Rodgers, Aaron
   broken collarbone, 62
   collision involving, 13
   as King of Hail Marys, 46–47
   unlearning motor learning by, 38
rotational motion, 8
rotator cuff injuries, 64
roughing the passer rule, 62
Ryan, Matt, **12**

San Diego Chargers, triangle training, 6
Sapp, Warren, 35
Sash, Tyler, 57–58
Seattle Seahawks, 41
shoulder pads, **53,** 53–55, 60
sidewinder kick, 49–50
Sigl, Craig, 41
skeletal muscles, 21
sliding friction, 15
slow-twitch (ST) fibers, 21, 23
Smith, Steve, 37
soccer-style kick, 49
spearing, 60
special relativity principle, 18
speed of light, 18
spinal cord injuries, 60, 61–62
Sports Illustrated (magazine), 47
Sproles, Darren, **17,** 17–19
St. John, Allen, 47
stamina, 24, 26–27
Starr, Bart, 33
Staubach, Roger, 40
Stingley, Darryl, 61–62, 65–66
strength training, 27–28
Stringer, Korey, 61, 64
Super Bowl 47, 5
Super Bowl 53, 8, 10–11
Swartz, Erik, 60
"Swatt, J.J.," 28

Tatum, Jack, 16, 61–62

77

Thomas Jefferson University, 63
throwing
    airborne behavior, 45–47, **46**
    shape and bounce of football and, 44–45
tonically active neurons (TANs), 38
torque
    ACL tears and, 63
    applying during tackling, 19, 50
    center of mass and, 7
    described, 17
training, **27**
    for agility, 29
    heatstroke and, 61, 64
    linemen, 29–30, **30**
    overall fitness and stamina, 26–27
    positive mental skills, 33
    practicing imagery, 41–42
    for quickness, 28–29
    for quick reaction time, 36–38
    school for kickers, 65
    skills drills, 30–31
    strength, 27–28
    triangle, 6
    unlearning skills, 38
    using virtual reality, 36–38
trajectory, 45
trash talkers, 35
traumatic brain injuries. *See* brain injuries
triangle training, 6
Tucker, Justin, **39,** 39–41
turf, 52–53

University of Maryland, 64

velocity, 11
Virginia Tech Center for Injury Biomechanics, 58–59
virtual reality (VR) technologies, 36–38
viscoelastic foam, 54
visualization, 41

Watson, Deshaun, 37–38
Watt, J.J., 28, 63–64
weight of players, 9, 56
work, described, 14

Young, Tavon, 63

PICTURE CREDITS

Cover: Aspen Photo/Shutterstock.com

5: Associated Press

10: Associated Press

12: Associated Press

17: Associated Press

22: TheVisualMD/Science Source

27: Arthur Eugene Preston/Shutterstock.com

30: Associated Press

34: Jeff Moffett/Icon SMI AAH/Newscom

39: Associated Press

42: Jordon Kelly/Icon Sportswire DHO/Newscom

46: Maury Aaseng

48: iStock.com/filo

53: Associated Press

58: Spencer Sutton/Science Source

62: Evan Oto/Science Source

66: iStock.com/ActionPics

ABOUT THE AUTHOR

Melissa Abramovitz is an award-winning author/freelance writer who specializes in writing educational nonfiction books and magazine articles for all age groups, from preschoolers through adults. She has published hundreds of magazine articles and more than fifty educational books for children and teenagers, along with short stories, poems, picture books, and resources for authors. Abramovitz graduated summa cum laude from the University of California, San Diego, with a degree in psychology and is also a graduate of the Institute of Children's Literature.